APPALACHIAN RACONTEUR

Poems from the Heart of Appalachia

By B H HAMILTON

APPALACHIAN RACONTEUR

By B H HAMILTON

Written by: B. H. Hamilton

Table of Contents

Table of Contents (cont.)

Table of Contents (cont.)

Table of Contents (cont.)

Table of Contents (cont.)

Table of Contents (cont.)

A Shoot from the Frost

Bright sounds deciphered without reference points are as unfocused as
yesterday's fog shrouded hollow-men trees standing at attention between
slumber and a renewal beginning amidst the frost.
The last days of a forgotten metaphor have fallen on the deaf ears of empty
corn cobs shredded of their memories by the crows of reaping patience from
the nadir of change at birth's gate lost.
Wailing lungs hurl accusations of change into the new air with shrill
protests against the shock of unimaginably new stimuli grating across
nerves accustomed to tranquil heartbeats' song.
The first confusion born of the hopefuls' act of love breaks forth from
incubation into a hallway of delivery leading to an unknown, responding to
promptings from necessity's thirty sixth belong.
Brilliantly blinded, momentarily side-winded against foreshadowed
happenstance, a new life force emerges at the announcement that a shower
may produce abundances of necessity things.
A first shocking swat from a latex enshrouded palm sends pain signals
racing to announce the first attempt at communication with the irrevocably
ignorant who barely grasp love's new wings.
Cold astonishment sends chill bumps first waves across newly emerged
wrinkled skin at naked bottom's adjunction with stainless steel cradles of
newborn scales at pencils' numbers graphite.
On white pages of electronic recorded vital statistic's inclusions of averages
mundane chores oft repeated by skilled hands to log love's first bloom of
certificates of being pardoned like Laffite.
From antiseptic imprisonment to infested blankets, hands, pacifiers, and
boiled rubber nipples of nourishment love becomes introduced to its first
reality check at the hands of indignant faults.

The learning curve, for newly birthed parents, moves sharply, arcing to the right and left but finally settling on an upward spiral into total gaga speeches of love's incongruent babble waltz.

Abnegate

Power was relinquished in order that footprints could mark the sands of the humble. Judgment was waived so that the guilty could walk holding hands with the innocent. Authority was laid aside to instruct the ignorant in the truth of faith, hope and Love. Eternity was cast behind for a brief moment so that healing could be sown in hearts. The sword was laid down and fishing nets were taken up to seine for the lost souls. Glory was yielded for an instant to allow the Living Word's message to propagate. The King of Kings momentarily abdicated his throne for the benefit of all mankind. Sovereignty was surrendered for a time for the Teacher to impart truth to the world. The Lord of Lord's crown was conceded for a coronet of cruel thorns that bled. Fellowship was abandoned at death to carry the sins of the world on Innocence. The life of the Incorruptible was handed over to the guilty to purge the condemned. Honor was forsaken for worn sandals and a peasant's robe of humility for inclusion. Garments were shed at the cross to bear witness to the prophets' testimonies past. Life was forgone at mid-season to allow the corrupt an opportunity to be healed. Shouts of Hosanna were discarded and cries of hate bellowed crucify, crucify him. God forbore the wrath of his judgment to allow the Word of his love to be slain for all. Sacrificed without guilt, Christ died for us all, but we must accept him unconditionally. As life was resigned, death entered the Guiltless and He sank into the tomb for us. Jesus abnegated his life once for all and to refuse his love is to crucify him again.

Adrift

Adrift in the seas of decision, we weigh future possibilities.

Adrift on the bay of triumph, we rejoice in right choices.

Adrift in the turmoil of trials, we struggle against our suffering.

Adrift on the ocean of discovery, we celebrate newness.

Adrift in the calm waters of complacency, we stagnate.

Adrift on the deep of revelation, we tremble at recognized truths.

Adrift in the marina of wealth, we forget our neighbor.

Adrift on the blue of acceptance, we share life.

Adrift in the waves of lewdness, we distort our love.

Adrift on the aqua expanse of repentance, we shine a lamp of hope.

Adrift in the surf of discontent, we wonder among lost souls.

Adrift on the fjords of grace, we are snatched from death.

Adrift in the icebergs of hate, we murder ourselves.

Adrift on the crimson waters of redemption, we see God's face.

Afar

Hope tendrils dimly twinkle from the cracks of the far voids.

Dark hints spring from the hairy creed covered remote anthropoids.

Green truth buds shoot from the fertility of distant soils.

Machiavellian soothsayers intrigue the unwary amidst future truth foils.

Archaic renditions of hope light the fuses of antediluvian prophecies.

Worm eaten tablet slanderers twist history with antique forgeries.

Apostle witnesses stand firm in testimonies of truth against the ancient iniquitous.

Contortionists twist bastions of stone half-facts to hide the far-flung nefarious.

Research of archaeological evidence corroborates the aged narrative of the disciples.

Narcotic smoke befuddles the weak as it is blown from the lips of historic misanthropists.

Wordsmiths build falling tetra blocks into mosaic billboards of certainty seen from afar.

Confusion rains snaring the malcontent in nets of lie-mongers' outlying propaganda altar.

Cartoonists of joy paint scenes of hope that fill the faithful to create love ties.

The tower of truth's steel girders are rust pitted by the onslaught of far off acid spittle lies.

Ajar

The doorway to eternal life only opens from within.

Thick bars and heavy chains of contention protect one's propensity to sin.

The wide-flung gate of innocence slams closed under the hand of treachery.

Case hardened bolts of rebellion are added to the door-face by debauchery.

The cause of our imprisonment is sought among the faces of strangers.

Nails of disobedience are anchored in the gate posts and lock in all dangers.

The rays of hope filter through cracks of love and try to burn holes in cloaks of hate.

Mud daubs of subversion chink the holes of grace and we select an evil fate.

The hands of redemption knock softly at the door with persistent implorations.

Earmuffs of guilt clamp out the sounds of freedom's explorations.

The words of grace are spoken against the oak timbers of contrition and unlock fear.

Timid fingers unbar the dungeons' doorway to find love near.

The tendrils of truth seep into open ears and oil the tumblers of admission.

Softly murmured repentance keys grate in rusted locks allowing submission.

The free offer of pardon breaks the bonds of enslavement and the meek submit.

Ajar, the opening is slight, but with innocence returned we are no longer unfit.

Anodyne

Our relief from all pain may be found in the aspirin droplets of thorn weeping's.

Our release from anguish was opened through the gates of the stripes of false beatings.

Our liberation from torment may be obtained under the palliative of pierced hands.

Our respite from sorrows was orchestrated by the conductor of the disciples' bands.

Our freedom from torture may be bequeathed by the analgesic tears of the Savior.

Our reprieve from grief was granted by sacrifice through the only Innocent's behavior.

Our ease from the ache of our burdens may be accomplished by the painkiller of grace.

Our unshackling from the chains of sin was wrought by the key upon the cross's face.

Our succor from death may be granted by accepting the anodyne of the Advocate's invitation.

Our acquittal is assured under the wings of the Dove of Peace giving the only salvation.

Arid

In the year of our Lord zero thirty-three,
the great redeemer Christ died for you and me.
He hung on the cross his followers thought it loss,
but victory was won and now we are free.
Our dull lives become an open book,
a silent picture show for God's eye to look.
We are sterile and useless striving and senseless,
but our victory is won all need freedom took.
A satire of hope, a flash of light,
an insipid small dust bunny of fright,
bromidic and choked we are withered and croaked.
But hope is sneaky, unshaken, and bright.
A dry branch is fallen cut from the vine,
it is barren, fruitless, and rated sub-prime.
Pedantic we grope in the dark without rope,
but a lifeline is free in God's time.
A weariful eye is cast to a Child,
whose life is given merciful, meek, and mild.
Arid hearts seek fate; a sign til time is late,

but a way is made to close the wild.

Axiom

Sayings of instruction are given for the benefit of all those who wish to listen. Truisms of life are written to plant seeds of possibility in the minds of the listening. Adages of correction are spoken in the plazas of wayward to bring about a reawakening to truth. Maxims of teaching are given in hopes that recognition may set in before perverseness becomes the norm. Aphorisms of admonition are repeated on the chalkboards of life to ingrain right lessons. Dictums of faith are expounded throughout papyrus scrolls of witnessing to bolster courage among the disciples. Proverbs of Solomon's wisdom are testimony to the decay of life after knowingly straying into the beds of seductresses of idolatry. Tenets of righteousness flutter on the frayed edges of torn hope offering glimpses of purpose. Axioms of God are engraved in the tablets of stone to remind us that obedience leads to a grace filled life and Love's open berth on the river of life.

Ballyhoo

The bellicose calf-casters bow down before earthly accomplishments and sway the wavering into acts of wrongdoing. The boisterous panderers thump the backs of the nefarious in congratulatory displays of validation cementing the parachutes of rationalization and the plunge is deadly. The unruly wayward herd the timid into corrals of acceptance and they mingle with the voracious and are consumed by the wicked. The belligerent egotistical perform self-worship rituals amid the open-minded and sedition expands into the hearts of the unprotected who succumb to temptation. The quarrelsome Lucifer recruiters entice the foolish with words and winks as they whisper encouragements of debauchery in the ears of the ever listening biddable. The petulant childish perform their temper tantrums on Broadway stages with tirades of profligacy to sway the patient from paths of correction. The cantankerous stir in the cesspools of immorality until the stench of wickedness fouls the air of the whole earth. The disobedient cling to their contentions of innocence in a ballyhoo of lies until the midnight hour is past and the sword of judgment descends.

Bedazzled

The shimmering luminescence of revelry entices untold numbers of the carnal sensory chasers into dreams of confusion. The brilliant sparkles of diamond effervescence hypnotize the ignorant into marriages of hate. The radiance of deceit permeates the veils of the gullible and they are easily stupefied into submission. The luster of copiousness impresses the covetous with offers of wealth beyond measure and they hoard their greed. The brightness of inclusion subverts the rebellious into gangs of stupefaction that war against truth. The gleaming shards of light seduce the sexually immoral between the bed-sheets of bewilderment and they succumb to the consequences. The iridescence of depravity shines about drawing in the moths of immoral acceptance and nations fall to accords of evil disguised as freedom. The robes of the angel of light bedazzle the unrepentant with free choices of earthly pursuits and billions are swayed into acts of attrition until the whole world becomes seduced.

Beguiling

Sweet words of honey fall on mesmerized ears and are embraced with open arms.

Whispered flatteries prickle hairs of joy along ego arms by the attractor's charms. Rose petals strewn before the feet of the haughty enthrall the glory fanatics. Brownie bites dangle enticement before the lips of the hungry glutton addicts. Incense sticks waft appealing aromas of incitement into the nostrils of the gullible. Kneading of the masseuse of depravity gives waves of pleasure to the malleable. Piping of the flute of dissipation draws in the dancing trance smitten deluded. Flashing color pallets from the disco ball of distortion are from pretty faces exuded.

Carousing belly dancers of seduction enchant the oblivious sensual chasing proud. Invitations of collusion are spread globally by media devoted to a consenting crowd. Flirtatious one-liners lure the lonely onto webs of deceit by a spell's hidden appeal. Lullabies composed of half-truths and lies fascinate the lost in dreams most surreal. Sideshows of immorality captivate the errant and lead them further into evil deeds. Illusions of opulence from the deceiver are beguiling the world into sowing sin seeds.

Blushing Roses

Bright faces glow from late spring cold winds blowing across zinfandel pastures freshly shorn. Fingerling buds pulse with tingling nerves and small hands pluck dew riddled daisies re-born. Wet sneakers paint tiny toes with kisses from chilly puddles along paths' winding middle trials. Muddy knees adorn running legs with opaque brown guesses by way of many mushy miles. Frayed elbows dangle threads of questions from the arms of quest seekers bounding over time. Earmuffs are skewed over misplaced sounds without muffled impertinences from envelop rhyme. Tattered pants' legs fly glory salutes after pounding calves laughing across a loamy field of joys. Runny noses announce happy lungs' bellowing life into little furnaces ablaze with lots of boys. Diamond drops sparkle verve from the dainty earlobes of nectarines gripped in a limb of swirls. Blushing lips of spirit radiate smiles from hearts of gladness skipping over grey slippers of girls. Fog tentacles play Beethoven concertos over stone keys and around brown tree stringed cellos.

Beings, in time and place, frolic with unfettered autonomy as a dance of delight trumpet bellows. Watery eyes squint questions across yards of last year's fallen memories into future days' launch. Afternoon sunbeams slice the fog of morning into pie pieces of yesterday's running haunch. Waltzes of growth spurts twirl gracefulness of spirit from toddlers to pre-school plantlets of hope. Bows on pigtails bounce up and down and hearts skip freely exuberances tilted to love's slope. Giggles chime in soft breezes sublime and days' light fades into hugs most tight and eyes sparkle. Transition beams fly under low clouds' embraces staining upturned cheeks a blurred pink archil. Cartwheel endings to toddlers' disinterest ushers curiosity through fading sun's re-birthed aurora. Proven impulsiveness is shed by a school door's open policy that folds fading truth's posh fedora. Expectant eyes slash questions through the windows of souls' modifications and pre-school starts. Practiced hands gently push timidity through the unknown nebula of educational sanity infarcts. Unseasoned moms jump headfirst into PTA's political agendas with hopes of children's acumen. Untried dads stride forth to conquer ignorance amidst hasty decisions that make us all human. Petals not yet opened, just a young bud above the thorn's lance reaching toward the next step up. Nourished by empathetic faltering attempts the young shoot swells into life's assessment cup.

Bound by Bond

The last antiseptic flicker from the frosted commercial florescent luminaries
waves a final goodbye.

Happy eyes crinkle over portrait splitting smiles wheeled to the curb of
future possibilities under a broken sky.

Bundled joy transported by a rubber-tired chariot to second beginnings
below jingling ceilings motion live Mobile.

Tests and trials by 2 AM cries, patience gropes along vines of learning to
find balance amidst chaos' ovule.

Nurtured by need and ever-growing awe, the heart expands to fill a void
unrecognized before a chosen plight.

Petals of enamored assistances slowly unfold as days sprout from the magic
beans of birth into a new light.

Loves lessons are slowly absorbed as a kindergartener's educations in
repeated confidences rebound.

A derelict's exhaustion from night watches' repetitiveness tolls a bell's
herald of bequeathed love crowned.

At last balanced on a knife's razor edge, the fully unfurled flower of truth by
love's fire is singing sleep.

First dawn, a bond stronger than welded steel beams is arced across the
small chinks bound in love's deep.

Boycott

The lines are drawn and the nefarious are armed with atomic bombs of inequity to slaughter and contaminate the citizenry of freedom. Sanctions are placed on the spreading of God's holy word in all public places to hasten the ripening of the fruits of immorality. An embargo against the free trade of truth is imposed by those in power to coerce the free thinkers into the mass will. The Redeemer's offer of arbitration has been rejected by the strikers against love to slay the ignorant. Marshall Law is the tool of choice of the arrogant used to proscribe the God-fearing from sharing their faith with the lost. The picketers against choice march day and night without wavering to block all attempts by Grace to enter contrite hearts. The Corner Stone of the world's castle of salvation is being pried out of the foundation by the impious' wrecking bar of strife to assure His rejection by the misled. The modern apostles of the Gospel's good news are being shunned by the prideful to imprison the truthful in attempts to limit the distribution of love. The open worship of God is being prohibited by the law interpreters to swing wide the gates of protection and let in the ravenous hordes of perversion vendors to allow the half dozen bad apples to spoil the bushel. The boycott of the Son of God is building a full head of steam and the riverboat of malice is filling with the betrayed souls of false reasoning.

Breach

Me and mine are blocks that tumble pain,
eyes focused in mirror's depth seek ill gain.
Shared neglect is a life lived large in regret.
To violate love caused irreparable stain.

Look and gape is to paint canvas's hate,
and a bow and bob evil thirst to sate.
A derelict's hole opens a flood to my soul
that stoops my back with a very heavy plate.

Ego blocks build walls of ice that twist into
a great spiral tower to heights of rue.
Winks and nods are tools of plundering mobs
used for malice's unerring vice goo.

Trespass feet tromp through icy roads of gloom,
as bonds of greed reel, us to our doom.
Law's infractions give deeds a cause for pause,
and breaches in faith transgress our boon.

Burnished

A sooty pot skewed between the ashes and the fire is blackened by the consequences of transgressions. A tarnished silver coin passed between the fingers of bribery slips into vice and becomes lost between the floorboards of greed. A barnacle covered hull that sails the murky waters of inequity is heavily weighted with guilt and eventually sinks to the bottom of the abyss. A diamond ring bound to the finger of a pig-herder of dissipation becomes layered in the filth of hedonism. The sword of injustice swung belligerently in the hand of the arrogant cuts a wide swath through the innocent and is blackened with their blood. The lantern-globe of enlightenment becomes opaque with the smoking oils of the covetous and its light fails. The window of opportunity is layered with the dust particles of decadence until there is no longer an outward view. The sooty pot, when scoured by the Brillo-pad of forgiveness, returns to obedience. The tarnished silver coin of bribery, when soaked in the blood of intercession, is re-invested in the bank of generosity. The barnacle covered hull of inequity, when scraped by the iron shackles of freedom, is re-routed to a destination of justice. The diamond ring of dissipation, when tumbled in the jewelry cleaner of clemency, sparkles with the new faucets of uprightness. The sword of injustice, when honed with the oil of honor, cuts with a blade of justice. The lantern globe of enlightenment, when polished with the cloth of truth, gives a strong light that guides the feet of the faithful onto the path of rectitude. The decadent layered window of opportunity, when burnished with the glass-cleaner of absolution, reveals the rewards of paradise.

Busy

Preoccupied with personal concerns, we squander our moments of precious time. Endeavors of daily tasks are used to fulfill desires for recognition and an easy dime. Captivated by the sparkle of the glass beads of disparity we consume others' lives. Enchanted by the opulence of neighbors' castles of sand we work for empty jives. Imbued with the weight of daily concerns we ignore the need to love our progeny. Distracted by news reports screaming our failings and their cost we fail homogeny. Engaged in time demanding contractual obligations we ignore others in great need. Misled by whispered misdirection we plod away from truth disdaining a good deed. Monopolized by the god of media-carnality we pay heed to falsehoods oft repeated. Enamored by scientists' ritual theorems, we salsa in ignorance till faith is depleted. Immersed in obsequiousness we pander to cruel masters who lash for a cheap thrill. Taken by gratifying tongues massaging our egos we use the guiltless to blood spill. Absorbed into the homogenous herd of normality we are utterly unified in deceits. Swirling through life on a curl of vapor we fail to see the fan of hate that defeats. Occupied by obligations too numerous to fathom we wade into quicksand and die. Cadence marching in rank upon rank puppets of atheists' hate and we ask not why. Engrossed with trivial self-styled tasks the time between twenty and ninety is brief. Floating on the breezes of chance we are snared on rose thorns like a dried leaf.

Busy we hustle and bustle the days away mommy cries are given a harsh reply.

Busy we crunch numbers with pain, as daddy pleads go unanswered and they cry.

Caboose

The disreputable locomotives pour out their smoke of inequity to cloud the view of their cupidity. The tender cars of bribery shovel the fuel of distortion into the firebox of greed powering the iniquitous. The freight cars of immoral desires are pulled into deeds of debauchery as they bind themselves to the liberal seditionist seductresses. The log trolleys of covetousness connect to the box cars of prosperity and unload profusions of debt to crush the needy. The petroleum tenders of insatiability are pulled along by the flat-cars of pride as they empty their energy for voraciousness into the waiting fires of the ignoble. The inclusive piggyback haulers of acceptance gather in the depraved and marry them to the gallows of the fuel tenders that ignite the fires of destruction. The coal cars of reprehension melded to the double decked diversion panderers fling the dust of coercion into the eyes of the wavering onlookers. The refrigerated cars of numbness coupled to the culpable temptresses ignore the lies of the malicious and become co-creators of strife. The car-haulers of vanity tied to the cold-hearted fame seekers exude vainglory and entice the covetous into acts of disobedience. The caboose of humility shackled to the train of superciliousness is dragged along through the mud of pomposity until the final Day of Judgment gives release into absolution.

Cerebral

Mistaken enlightenment of the damned confounds the lies of the obtuse as they pander to unholy lusts. The Id mongers cater to the hedonistic to validate feelings of inadequacy in corroborations of wrongdoing. Convincing whispers of unholy desires deceive the ignorant into pursuing hinted pleasures through inveigled reactions. Egotistical indulgent right-brain swingers exude simplistic illogical conclusions of tarnished emotion into media splattered subliminal corruptions of truth. The reactionary thinkers utilize feelings of inadequacy to confound the wise with volumes of idiocy propaganda. The freedom believers revel in their ability to support only their own freedoms while removing all from the grasp of their left brained brothers and sisters. Impressionists of delusion paint intricate masterpieces of distortion to confound the illiterate into acts of duplicity. Pugnacious psychological assassins war against the battlements of righteousness until holes are punched into the armor of respectability. Subversions by hidden law phrases undermine the foundation blocks of greatness until the entire castle of hope implodes onto the shoulders of the tolerant and the eagle is slain. Cerebral analysis is ignored by the conspirators of debauchery until the statistical analysis machine happens to support their own theories of evolution and scientific happenstance chitty-chitty bang-bang spontaneous life eruptions.

Coaxed

Charmed by flattery and pride the errant chase after celebrities and are enslaved in chains of blind infatuations. Cajoled by sycophantic melodies of enticement the immature are rounded-up into orchestras of sophistry admirers. Persuaded by eloquent speeches from swindlers of truth the spiritually frail submit their throats to liars' manipulations and become effectual tools of evil. Enticed into acts of wantonness the decadent take self-indulgence to heights of depravity while declaring they are free of responsibility and exempt themselves from all consequences. Wheedled by covert messages from decades of media hype the duped are hypnotized into acquiescent stupors and drool on their couches of indifference. Sweet talked by the serpents of mendacity the compliant are molded into clerical emissaries of malice. Won over by eloquent speeches of the haughty the pompous join the ranks of confusion and revel in ignorance. Beguiled by offers of opulence the miserly board the cruise ships of wealth and sail into the waters of greed from which there is no return. Wooed by the scantily clad prostitutes of infidelity the sexually immoral are enamored into lewd acts of sedition. Enthralled by power brokers' influences the egotistical jump on the band wagon of the proud and blow their own horns of vanity. Coaxed onto the road to perdition by the carrot of knowledge the feet of the unwise inch slowly forward until the approach to the final brink crumbles under their wayward feet and they fall.

Crawlspace Clues

From cradle to floor is a small reach for man, but a multi-hour flight for the infant in charge. Unlocked opportunity beckons the explorer's zeal onto new highs and motives are no longer hampered by the imprisonment of crib protections for parent's security falsehoods bolstered. Curious carpet liaisons of softly whispered possibility find knees and buttocks well cushioned above air-ride shocks of fluff, but feet pound out frustrations in bongo thumps muffled attention. Bolstered efforts provide movement rewards upon much practiced rolls and wiggled skirmishes of brittle pardons give way too much wailing when bare knees find the reality of hard floor's ice. Florets of golden eye crinkles accompanied by bouts of giggles at nothing elicit parents' coos and warm hugs reward errors when little chins strike surprises and cries of bad discovery echo. Futility repetitions soon meld into cry-wolf learning that slowly lessens hugged rewards simile as learned withholdings mount after failed swindling tries from the A-team benefactor by detection. The vines of temptation must be skillfully and cautiously pruned to cultivate the new shoots into the light of advantages within love's constraining corrections to avoid death's knock. The first reality check of adoration comes swiftly on the heels of trials by envelop pushing that test the boundaries of safety zones, but unhampered instinct takes control and restrains liberalism. From cradle to floor the journey begins circumscribed by love's guidance and the timid gradually feel the way past limitations of inexperience by way of helping hands whispered encouragements. Boot camp stints asphalt the winding highway to toddlers' spurts toward the goal of pre-school by way of irresistible employment of guidance missteps corrected at right angled growth charts. Hearts grow ten sizes as little knees fly across pastures of mission control rooms filled with advice from educated oblivion by those who hold no clue to the love of children that are absence. Experience explosions rocket down from the lips of Grandma and Grandpa without invitation or willingness to listen by reluctant moms and pops who would rather embrace mistakes despite the cost. Ignoring the full bloom of love's maturation to bolster pride in self-absorption makes wobble the legs of professionalism infarcts of loathing of help needs from the well-rehearsed aid. The early springtime of dawn of new life holds critical waypoints on the GPS of love's underappreciated destinies that await determination amid adversities innumerable stacked against mom. From womb to toddler as a seed to seedling careful nurturing is a must to insure immeasurable well-rounded maturation to the point of absorbing love's eternal flame into the heart of a hopeful. Balanced between futility and harm, infants' hearts and minds must be watered by the April showers of both trial and error and the experience of wrinkled hands' unconditional love offerings.

Crisis

On the brink we stand, breaths held awaiting the consequences of our evil acts. Closed door secret enclaves hide the deliberate subversion of domestic enemy pacts. Law is ignored by tyranny prostitutes fornicating in arrogant Napoleonistic decrees. Psycho-manipulation is propagated by media wands waived by the fairy vortices. Freedom to choose has been seized by the usurpers of the founding fathers' fidelity. Third world despots bind their Machiavellian values on the slaves of incredulity. Subverted wisdom is used to confound the simple minded with perverse adages. Tantrums by illicit youth place stockades on all and lock them in immoral bondages. Business policies embrace voracity and the poor languish in shadows of the spited. Religious doctrines pervert the truth into salacious satires to appease the slighted. The albatrosses of disobedience hang in anvil necklaces on the necks of hosts. Grandiose revelries play out amidst the inundating swarms of illicit aimless ghosts. Decadence swirls in mists of unawareness as blasphemies pour from lips uncouth. Looming across the stratosphere the crisis of finality of delusions ends in truth.

Crossed

Crossed between the stars of fate battling to relieve the bonds of hate.

Crossed between the knots of time struggling to unravel the maze of a confused mind.

Crossed between the edges of the earth searching for the answers since birth.

Crossed between the two arms of exclusion holding firm the gates of confusion.

Crossed between the rails of fear fleeing away from the train of tears.

Crossed between the cities' boroughs cringing from the rich man's sorrows.

Crossed between ships of passion steaming toward goals of the lowest fashion.

Crossed between the legs of inequity slashing with knives trying to shred ambiguity.

Crossed between the rocks of ages grinding together hope lost in lurid pages.

Crossed between the rivers of life struggling in the currents of strife.

Crossed between the oceans' hues swimming through the haze of ten thousand blues.

Crossed between the fallen trees of crime rapping out the basest ryhme.

Crossed between the grains of sand drowning in the image of the promised land.

Crossed between the carnal pleasures pursuing lusts with all our endeavors.

Crossed between the lies repeat swayed into running toward defeat.

Crossed between the ropes of freedom swinging along in darkness of our putrid kingdom. Crossed between the interstates' span driving through the fog of earthly man.

Crossed between the truth of grace fleeing from our Redeemer's face.

Crossed between the teeth of death fallen when we take our very last breath.

Crossed, crossed, crossed we have chosen to be now lost.

Crust

We are created transparent so that light pours into our souls and darkness flees. Encased in a cocoon of time opaqueness grows clouding our eagerness to please. We sow seeds of desire and pursue them into murky waters and the film thickens. Finely cultivated weeds of aspirations grow choking out the light and sin quickens. We step from the paths of righteousness and sink into the quicksand of malice. Ignoring the Windex of correction we fall into soot-coated rooms chasing a chalice. We wallow in the slime of immorality with the iniquitous and the mud dries. Crawling out into the rays of hope all light is reflected except from our open eyes. We squeeze tight the windows to our soul to hide reprehensible acts of duplicity. Lying in word and act the depraved seek shelter from the truth's solid simplicity. We walk in shadows to avoid exposure to veracity that may sloth off our debris. Blaming everyone else for our dilemma we avoid liability and hide in fake filigree. We embrace offenses and armor evil with recurring pride marches to uphold a lie. Hating the voices of truth the guilty call them haters and stone them in a nasty vie. We portend our own end by acts of our hands and words of our lips and earn lashes. Baking in the fires our own building we harden our facades into burned crusts that crumble into deathly ashes.

Cryptic

On the sands of strange shores hope wrecks sit,

while psalms of renewed faith stones are writ.

Omens dark and seductive lure a dim mark,

as proverbs' ward peals warning shots bit.

On the shores of vague duplicity imps wait,

while broken lives seek redemption's gate.

Augurs most obscure stain robes with isolate pain,

as secretive conclaves meet of fate.

On the coasts of unclear choices waves toss,

while axioms teach and count wise the loss.

Foretelling unclear bode ill debates in code,

as murky waters cover the forgotten cross.

On the beach of Delphian ill words spill,

while adages recount woes of grist mill.

Predictions of woe encrypt hate to sow,

as cryptic songs herald a time to kill.

Curative

In need of healing, we stab ourselves to death.

Without a remedying we struggle with a broken breath.

In need of restoration, we ooze with self-inflicted damage.

Without a vulnerary we decay into cesspools of carnage.

In need of a helpful hand, we smite the offer of it.

Without a sanative aide we are entrapped in an insane fit.

In need of a benefactor, we continually slay the Redeemer.

Without a salutary instructor we sail on a darkness steamer.

In need of a wholesome guide, we flee words of correction.

Without the proper curative we die horrendously without protection.

Dabble

Just a stroll across the meadow to taste the turbulent waters on the other side tempts. Just a spoonful of decadence and sugar's seduction fills the senses with guilty joy. Just a quick romp between the sheets of fornication and no one will see death's face. Just a short reach into your neighbor's garage a new tool to borrow, he will not miss. Just a little white lie on the stand to shift responsibility and no one will be the wiser. Just a sip or a shot or two is okay and excused drunken actions are soon overlooked. Just a sample of nose candy is become the accepted norm of the jet-setting vagrants. Just a mild beating for the disobedient spouse is permissible if you don't get caught. Just a bow or two before the idols of indulgence and greed claims the weak willed. Just a peek at the table of divination and the future's delights unfold to the blind. Just a zip on the dance floor with the perverse to see what may be missed corrupts. Just a handful of gold swindled from the poor builds the miser's tower to opulence. Just a paragraph printed lie to slightly mislead costs a million souls a word of truth. Just a dabble with sin seems a simple indulgence but once the crack of the abyss is opened there is but one way out and it is not by your own power.

Devoured

Consumed by daily concerns, freedom is abandoned for imprisonment in idolatry. Buried in responsibilities of chosen futility, we founder in bosomed obligations. Obsessed with gaining the whole world at any cost before death, we forget to live. Overwhelmed by schedules of innumerable pointless acts, we sell our children's souls to the media pedophiles.

Engulfed in fires of passion for affluence, we use all means to hoard material decay. Drenched in the blood of the scapegoats of political prostitutes, we drown in the vomit of contentious falsehoods. Demolished with the twin towers of avarice and odium, we ignore the cries of the socially isolated and they starve.

Assassinated truths are dropped into the desolate trenches of denunciation and become forgotten. Conquered by acquiescence, morality is rolled from the guillotine of acceptance into a cesspool of indulgence. Used up by seamstresses of party swaddling clothes, the threads of liberty are frayed into unrecognizable string-balls of chaos. Consumed by the ravenous appetite for depravity, the Constitution is defecated into putrid piles of ignorance.

Relinquished by hands of fear, freedom is buried under rock catacombs of policy. Torn to shreds by politicians' molars of pride, the people's choices are masticated into palatable pulp for the tyrants' pleasures. Devoured by the zombies of falsehood, truth and justice are offensive to the misled goats as the willingly enter the slaughterhouse.

Divided

Divide and conquer the oldest ploy of the battlefield is unfolding before our eyes. To the victor go the spoils rings in the hammer blows at the final close of the coffin. Doctrines of man inspired by Lucifer are imbedded in the fabric of truth and make stains of schism among the troops.

The warnings of God are ignored by the pretentious rift teachers of hollow dogma. Approval of lies and clasping evil to the bosoms of tolerance opens the gates to loss. The word of truth stamped in the hearts of the righteous is cut out by subversive media knives thrown from subliminal scabbards.

The culpable roam freely among the parishioners whispering seductive temptations. Clay facades of hypocrisy coat the fangs of destruction with rose petals of discord. Hatred wears the masks of validations repeated in pride marches of the fallen ones. Murderers don the plastic safety tips of rapiers to give a false sense of security to the intended victims of assassinations of hope.

Embraces of secularism infiltrates the ranks of the weakly religious dilettantes. Security guard priests take bribes from seditionists opening windows of access. Enemies flood through the castle breaches and attack at will among the ignorant. Blindly divided without awareness of the dividers the armies of salvation have been turned toward the chasm transgressions' consequence and embrace death's tendrils.

Dole

Distress lies in a yoke of lead around the necks of the willful and its weight crushes. The gravity of the galaxy of trepidation spins a black-hole from which none escape. The missiles of blame roar outward in harsh words but soon annihilate the accusers. The trout of sorrows is on the hook and we reel it in as quickly as a falling meteor. The symptoms of evil are evident in the pustules of self-loathing hidden behind lies. Despondence lurks in the shadows cast by oppression and is ignored at great cost. The eyes of the world seek the gates to happiness by probing among shadows of sin. Miserably alone standing amid seven billion miserable others we weep. Embraced in the arms of contention the astronauts of false hope are honored by ego. The voices of disobedience whisper sweet enticements in the ears of the validators. Oeuvres of the stars are played by harps of bribery and lure the oblivious into ruin. The Day of Judgment is descending as quickly as a comet from Jupiter's shadow. Our lusts remain embedded in idolatry and wantonness until death's gates open. The wage of hatred is earned in full and at the final hour an accounting is due. Scales of justice are from the deep to the peak and debt is heavier than all but grace.

Drogher

Life's full burdens go unrecognized by the willful as they unload them on others. The caravan of guiles plods heavily laden with lotuses through the desert of illusion. The sides of the train of consternation bulge with a mob of errant simpleton cohorts. Faithless shirkers shed responsibility in heaps of cast-off cicada shells of duplicity. The ship of opulence goes down in the ocean of denial sunk by a worldly hoard. The Airbus of the haughty flies above the clouds of humbled and into the abyss. Folly takes hold of the unwise and blindly leads them along paths to destruction. The castle towers of condescension reach heavenward but the foundation is of clay. The fields of the wheat of discord are choked by the thorns of conflict and wither. Obstreperousness is now pandemic and its symptoms are a ponderous yoke to all. The mouths of contention voice harsh words of condemnation that weigh heavily. The tentacles of persecution wrap around the meek and seek to crush the truth. Mendacity is overflowing from the lake of ineptitude and the flood covers the earth. The feet of murderous legions trample the nonconformists stomping out freedom. The arms of temptation embrace and coax the weak willed into the bastilles of sin. Forgiveness resides with the giver of grace through pardon by our true Intercessor. The acceptance by an open-door policy through free will is the only answer to death. The Drogher of our onerous burden of guilt is sufficient to carry all condemnations.

Dubious

Of questionable repute grain of salt,

words to mislead even the most stalwart.

The father of lies sends emissaries and spies,

to warp and bend truth until we are caught.

Of doubtful origin sent acts to stain,

deeds, endeavors hand us over to pain.

The seducer of the weak leads to ill speak,

give soft songs of iron cast out to gain.

Of suspect motive led to alter life,

and throats bared to the evil call to knife.

The slayer of the open-minded paints greyer,

bleak scenes and gives hopeless immoral strife.

Of dubious design a quilt crime,

woven pattern tale of a wicked time.

The dictator of revelry tax raised axe,

blind result death's knell gives a last rhyme.

Ductus

The handwriting on the wall is engraved by the hand of the ignorant who scribble. Fanciful calligraphy swirls the ink of life in sprays across canvases of the ignoble. The algorithmic scripts of the haughty impress the life slates of the easily deceived. Elegant longhand links the fool's lies into strands of web snaring the not reprieved. The penmanship of subversion authors laws of treachery reeling in fish ignorance. Chic-lit chirographies paint abstract outlooks open to interpretations of petulance. The fists of opulence beat cryptic hieroglyphs into the clay tablets of the enslaved. Capricious hands scroll subliminal inducements across screens of the app-raved. The ductus of hate betrays the unwary who listen to the melodies of the lotus flower.

Ebony

Atramentous hearts beat in all chests, yet respecters-of-person point fingers. Haughtiness exudes from the acts of the unwise and they demean their neighbor. Raven cries shoot arrows of hate from the lips of bigots piercing all in their paths. Envy wraps layers of cellophane around our covetousness and we forget our lives. Onyx thoughts absorb all light and muddy accusations are hurled in all directions. Blame for ancient wrongs is moored in the harbor of cynical hearts that decay. Sable cloaks are used to hide Machiavellian plots from the eyes of correction. Jealousy of alleged advantages oozes green contagious fog into valleys of peace. Jet crusts are burned over the pastries of brotherhood and gangs war against family. Pride builds walls of exclusion barring light from entering the gates of separation. Inky smoke is blown from racist's pipes and shadows the new sprouts with hatred. Separatism locks shackles of renewed bondage to lies to raise armies of entitlement. Pitch-dark caverns are opened with keys of distortion leading to empires of sedition. Despondency releases dandelionian seeds of mistakenness onto breezes of turmoil. Black ops are conducted at midnight to cover acts of selfishness from our own eyes. Genocide swords cut the throats of all since Homo is the only human genus. Ebony cores are under all Homosapiens' skins and all like Adam are accountable. Grace entered the earth through death and pardon walked side-by-side with guilt. Ivory shines from only one face and the Redeemer is all that can whitewash ebony.

Emanate

The love of God should spring forth from the hearts of Christians and shine for all. The hope of grace should flow from the wellsprings of faith and reverberate in joy. The peace that surpasses understanding should proceed out of our living examples. The testimonies of the twelve apostles should issue solid verdicts to discredit the lie. The changed heart should rise up from the ashes of condemnation to share the light. The willingness to serve should be derived from a desire to spread love to the world. The message of salvation should originate with honest orations of Christ's motives. The intent of ministers should stem from humbled mind-sets reflected in actions. The brotherhood of the saints should commence to draw all lost souls to contrition. The offspring of perseverance should start the wayward on the homeward journey. The correction of wrong should come from the loving experience of the forgiven. The example of Jesus should emerge from the love of all and manifest in servitude. The Good News of the gospel should begin everyone's day with abundant richness. The magnetism of unbound joy should emanate from the lives of the redeemed.

Epiphany

Recognition of truth is freely given to those who seek it diligently as a miser a coin. An iridescent mirage plays a concerto of seduction before the eyes of the deceived. Acknowledgement of love opens the doors of the heart to enlightenment of spirit. Scarlet pretense curtains veil the sight of the pompous materialistic smoke jumpers. Conceding one's need for atonement frees the bonds of enslavement to delusion. Softly whispered enticements lead the wayward into pastures full of bitter deaths. Discernment floats into the minds of all on butterfly wings of grace that pleads. Pride expels the suggestions of need from the thoughts of the nefarious by attrition. Intuition points the feet of the cautious onto paths lined with the rose petals of hope. Counsel from the rebellious bends the ears of the willful leading to ignorant revelry. Observations of faithfulness open the ears of the seeking to melodies of instruction. Distortions of freewill ring a cacophony of vulgarity on the eardrums of the defiant. Revelation shines forth a beacon of guiding light to lead all eyes to the rejoicing. Concealment of truth rolls a cloudbank of ignorance across the light of redemption. Sudden awareness of one's plight swings wide the door of salvation letting love in. Accusations of guilt oil the deadbolts of separation snapping the locks of refusal. Epiphany comes to souls whose guilt prison has been unlocked by scarred hands.

Escrow

Stewards only we misuse all that our eyes behold even our own mirror's image. Short-term tenants we purposefully try to steal ownership from our Benefactor. Custodians of bodies on loan we claim unmitigated rights erroneously stolen. Caretakers' duties ingrained in the mitochondria of every cell's glory we ignore. Lessees that waste all opportunities given by the Master of the garden we neglect. Holders in trust of our temples, our breath, and lives that we live we squander time. Overseers of a good creation we abuse neglect and ravage until only ashes remain. Managers of the estate of our dream we exploit every opportunity of our charges. Minor investors in the stock market of hope we selfishly defraud all others. Entrusted with the privileged duty of the good news we subjugate the oppressed. Keeper of the property of the Most High we usurp authority and abandon duty. Concierges of God's holy temples we prostitute our lives to the biggest tippers. Trustees of our neighbors' inheritances we pilfer all assets until nothing remains. Sharecroppers in the garden of Love we tend to brambles and let the crop wither. Glorious miracle held in escrow until the return of the rightful Owner is our charge. What will be our defense at the Owner's return? Silent graves of the guilty lie in waiting.

Esprit de corps

Repaired fellowship succor to the lost,
who seek openly to mend severed ties' cost.
Sutured loyalty sews tears of remorse fears
into the fabric of humble faith fixes crossed.

Healed fervor appends the wise to grace,
that paves a straight path to a won race.
Restored devotions lead to praise commotions
that pour out hymns to a glorious face.

Cured ills give rise to stolid passion acts,
that herd the lost into pens of safe pacts.
Cemented cracks bind woes to stone repelling foes,
who splinter false dogma against the facts.

Knitted camaraderie gives chance to bond
that is broken but of we are fond.
Esprit de corps to morality is no bore,
as a rock key, an arch's strength don.

Expiate

Guilt's weight crushes the oppressed under a self-inflicted burden of resentment. Atonement awaits a contrite heart's cry for absolution through humble repentance. Flesh's desires stone the will into submission into slavery manipulated by hate. Restored fellowship is gifted to truly repentant hearts seeking shelter in the Savior. Condemnation's chains bind tightly the spirits of the disobedient ensnaring them. Repaired relationships are sewn together by the awl stitches of crucified Love. Accusation's whispered testimonies snap shut the stockade of self-incrimination. Compensation has been paid for the accrued debts of those who freely accept it. Indictment's hammer wields a heavy blow to the heads of Machiavellian purveyors. Counterbalanced by intercession the scales of justice tip in favor of the pardoned. Wage's payments earned through deceit and sedition are death and separation. Outweighed by the blood drops of pure Love unification is restored by grace. Judgment's verdict against the treasonous will come against all the unrepentant. Expiated by the blood of grace by acceptance the sentence of believers is expunged.

Exuviate

The soiled long-johns of self-absorption must be discarded before a
disinfected

white robe can be donned.

The excretions of debauchery must be sloughed from the garments of
carnality by

grace before cleanliness can be honed.

The pinfeathers of falsehood must be molted before the new armor of
righteousness may be allowed to shine with a pure light.

The cloak of darkness must be cast away before the door handle of
forgiveness may

be turned letting in the Right.

The top hat of partiality must be doffed to the seemingly unsavory before
the

blindness of hypocrisy may be lifted.

The harness to sin must be taken off before the recognition of slavery is
embraced

and the freedom of truth can be gifted.

The fetters of avarice, hate, wantonness, depravity, and covetousness must
be

slipped with the aid of one Mediation.

The investments in self-fulfillment must be divested to step foot onto the path to joyous liberation.

The ways of deceit must be exuviated before the wholeness of Love can enter

contrite hearts and work away strife.

The reigns of control must be dropped into the hand of the Omniscient to

obtain the very best of life.

Fabric

Essences of life abide in Love until conception when it settles in flesh for glory. Emanations of peace flow into willing hearts as they grow toward things of spirit. Frameworks of hope support the weakness of the flesh transcending lies unto life. Compositions of joy weave together acceptors of truth through a loom of transition. Patterns of uplifting fill the hands of the willing as they give comfort to the lost. Essentials of faith swirl in tendrils of sustenance by prayers of the self-sacrificing. Structures of enlightenment pour out the good news of the Living Word to all ears. Schemes of fruitfulness fertilize the vine of life nurturing the branches to produce. Beings of instruction settle in the minds of listeners and whisper encouragements. Constitutions of correction adjust the waywardness of contrite hearts and heal them. Fabrics of intercession torn from Christ hold back hate filled indictments of Satan.

Fall Upward

Orange, red, yellow, brown many vibrant color pallets abound.

Every October the trees bloom with death, only choice places found.

The warmth of the rays melts through the mists onto golden carpets.

Sparkly crystals twinkle as ghost tendrils of steam swirl into misty turrets.

Lowly, golden glistening tears of dew on a leaf, there are so many uses for thee.

Dog's bed, mulch for the flowers and a child's crunchy window are for all to see.

Slumber, nap, death's practice, no matter; the trees are quiet this season.

Neighbors glare and mutter only work they see, beauty escapes them no reason.

Through a child's eye we must walk, frolic for the joy to partake.

Red as aunt Tildy's hat, yellow as a banana; we may stop and appreciate.

The children are much wiser, if only we could tell, begin to listen.

Orange as a Jack-o-lantern's face, frost sparkles more than diamonds glisten.

Our time of breath is much shorter than the mighty Oak tree.

We squander it with worried fate; better to sing a colorful shower and be free.

Rake, rake, rake no time to think, no time we cannot partake in the fun.

Stop, smell, listen a moment, for time is a precious gift; feel the warm sun.

A golden whirlwind about us dances, to join in is blissful.

If we stand and stare, do not embrace; we are only wishful.

What will the neighbors think we ask; locked in indecision?

A child never considers these weighty matters; no uncertainty, just precision.

To twirl is bliss, to jump a joy, so why not dive in simple ecstasy.

With rake in hand, sweat running down our noses, backs ache in agony.

No way to recognize our plight is of our own making.

The pleasure is there, the fun waits by the way; free for our taking.

If only we could let go, dive right in; simple joy we would find.

Opinions we consider, however hands to the rake, ourselves we bind.

A shower of color, a shower of laughter around us floats.

All we must do is let go, shed our imprisonment from our coats.

Family

Family is a network of love working together for the good of all its members.

Family loves unconditionally hugging through pain and faults to reconciliation.

Family breaks the rules of blame, retribution, and vengeance.

Family gives hope in times of despair.

Families bind the claws of hate to keep out evil's grasp.

Families give freely of time and listen to the voices of pain.

Families play games for children's delight, nurturing and sharing love's patience.

Families hold hands in chains of strength binding weak links onto the solid anchor of love.

Family unclasps an unwilling link, freeing it to flee from love's embrace.

Family sends out strings of renewal to make available strands of forgiveness, if sought.

Family sees across diversities in culture, politics, and opinions bridging a gulf of division. Family is bound fast together, not by blood or similarities.

Families give wings to dreamers.

Families open the doors of opportunity to the timid.

Families embrace the differences that would oft rend apart.

Families tie the world with ribbons of yellow empathy, a reason for humanity's redemption.

Family worldwide, if only we would open all our eyes to truth, acceptance, and love, freely shared with everyone.

Ferns 'n Fairies

The magic is for a child's eyes alone hidden from the cynicism of adults.

The green light fairy dust floats in the dreams of the incorruptible, pure ones.

Innocence lost, blinds, binds a hollow loss unrecognized voices harsh full of insults.

The children all know love concurs opens eyes of righteousness cherish daughters and sons.

At what point fallen, ceased recognition, sightless seeing without reason or delight?

Foolishly we demand reality, imaginations crushed, hopes shredded, dreams riven.

They jump and titter at our foolish demand but with age and whittling we mold their fright.

Every child fights a good fight but parents persist, slowly consume fantasies no quarter given.

Adults see nothing but childhood games to be outgrown, delivered from, saved for sanity's sake.

Most every child's eyes are closed by dark reasoning reality choking down dreams razed.

Ferns 'n Fairies delight the senses dreams fly behind stars a child points a path we cannot take.

If only adults' eyes would open love would claim all in a blessed embrace how we would be amazed.

Gifts of joy abound the children all know to cherish, partake rejoice in magic's glow.

They strive to make us see joys their eyes alone behold our hands they grasp and lead.

Tree limbs and moss our steps crush down last year's leaves are all we see are minds too slow.

Look, little fingers point right then left, tree trunks and shadows, but there is more they plead.

The more we smile condescending quirks the harder they try, little tears roll, recognition sets in.

A little child can clearly see our blind limits, the walls we built around our sight ages past.

Ferns 'n Fairies are for little eyes only such wonders we hide from run from through briar 'n fen.

It's okay Daddy, little words console give comfort knowing the blindness prohibits, holds fast.

Fescennine

Offensive slander of the morally stolid is now the new standard of persecution. Coarse swine trample the pearls of warning into the filth of the sty of the iniquitous. Scurrilous lies are shot from the bows of educated stupidity and pierce the humbled. Foul nefarious flesh drunkards swill their own vomit then spew it onto the forgiven. Lascivious aphorisms fire off the tongues of the egocentric and scorch grace. Vulgar scavengers rend the fallen removing all hope for reconciliation with Love. Obscene denigrations are hurled from the catapults of partiality and crush the just. Lurid marauders ravage the scant possessions of the poor and rape their hard work. Indecent proposals are set in contracts of immorality formed to enslave the weak. Filthy walking dead grope the wavering to seduce them into damnation's purview. Salacious speeches pour from the mouth of persuasion to assemble death's victims. Crude wordsmiths craft subliminal messages of caricature to woo the party minded. Raunchy melodies soar from the throats of provocative sirens to lure the gullible. Fescennine candles' lights cast shadows among the dancing condemned to death.

Final Frontier

Space we're told is the last unexplored realm the final frontier to discover from earth.

Though we have barely splashed the surface of the deep which science says gave us birth.

From carbon, nitrogen of chemicals they tell life erupted from nothing they cannot explain how.

Nine hundred years ago science told us mice spontaneously appeared from dirty clothes wow.

We trust blindly still nothing learned in nine hundred years ignorance is bliss the masses all know.

Forward into the dark ages we leap with great joy believing lies too lazy to seek truth whoa.

Backward evolving could it be we return soon to be no more than monkeys in a tree.

Scientists blinded by the ends decided determined before studied so ignorantly free.

From monkey to unknown mammal, we are told the reversion continues till back an age we go.

Time speeds up like a clock in hyper drive the stars flash by millions of years to change if so.

The scientists all buckle us in their bubble of lies the train of their theory provides a great ride.

This point our cousins join us again rats and marsupials and such where now human pride?

The meek shall inherit the earth one day soon to be tailless amphibians slithering in muck.

Next to sea we return something like a fish with legs we are told, where's the link, doesn't it suck?

Slithering, squirming soon a fish we are to be with gills do not you know, what year 265 million BC?

What came before the fish, an amoeba, bacterium, coral who can say not science, ice unfreeze?

Back to the primordial soup we have now slithered spot of nitrogen, dab of carbon, sulfur drop core.

Science's final frontier finally achieved what better to be than a dab of muck on the ocean's floor?

Flux

Obstinate inert alloy floating in the void without purpose is strong but useless. Precious gems buried in a seam of ore under a mountain are striking but worthless. Fine gold locked in thick quartz is untarnished but can buy no peace for the wicked. Nectar of life fixed in the tightly closed petals of the surly wild rose slacks no thirst. Fruit of knowledge of good and evil opened eyes but disobedience earned death. Blood from beasts shed for atonement paid a provisional fee for remission of sin. The blending of an alloy requires a catalyst to meld the metals into a useful tool. The color of topaz must have intense heat from a furnace to surpass its opaqueness. The gold quartz must be milled to release its precious metal for use in the market. The wild rose needs sunlight to coax open its petals to allow access to life's nectar. The wages of sin necessitate death to the unrepentant in payment of debts owed.

The flux of punishment mandates a pure sacrifice to wash away the guilt of rebelliousness.

Foible

Vices of the flesh entice the weak willed into nefarious acts of self-indulgence. Flaws of the character leak morality from the cracks made by blows to hearts. Demerits continuously assaulted into the ears of despair lead to fractured minds. Imperfections in the armor of faith allow darkness to seep in and gain access to fear. Weaknesses of the carnally minded draw their feet into actions of hate peddling. Deficiencies in the belief of truth draw the lies of the obtuse into the herd mentality. Failings of the forgiven are used to support the mendacity of the perverse of mind. Shortcomings of our neighbors are the basis for our rationalizations of our inequity. Sins of others are sharpened in forges of condemnation and the swords sever family. Faults of friends are baked in ovens of blame and the bricks lay walls of hypocrisy. Bad habits of ministers entice fault seekers to denunciate truth leading to defeat. Eccentricities of the famous sway the idolatrous into immoral acts of depravity. Quirks of celebrities entice the simple minded into atrocities against nature's order. Foibles pour out of humans paving the easy path to destruction with copious lies.

Fragments

Fragments of time wasted in bickering fall despondently into dust. Shattered seconds are splintered icicles struck with a sledgehammer of hate. Time fragments are found in the crevices between the ancient sand grains on the beach. Washed among the whispers of the jellyfish they give testimony to the fall. Fragments of love misguided lead to the cataracts of lust. Eon's maw has swallowed us all into the inky blackness of desires pursued. Fragments of life lived out in hastily forgotten memories of sacrifice fall on deaf ears. Fractured by the pursuing of elusive hardly recognized endeavors of futility we flounder. Bits of royal purple cloth float with the dust mites of eternity's glorious concentric worship. Jagged bits of the age taste like bitter coffee dregs spilled from the pot into our cups of inequity. Gritty fragments of our failures haunt us through our purposeful pursuits of joy. Stardust glitters golden on the fall of time's hammer striking a final blow on the glacier's last bastion. Time fragments have been scattered like daisy petals torn loose before their time by tiny fingers of hope. Riven conclave of laughter applauds the fate of the lost among enticing gem fragments of delusion. A new quilt block of pattern is made ready to be sewn into the fabric of the universe by the ancient hands of Love. Millennia fragments foster the last two thousand years of hope washed onto the shores of life offered to the humble lost. Searched and found wanting fragmented lies whispered among ancient stones ears seduced millions. Babel's legacy of ignorance and striving metamorphosed into the desolation of abomination constructed minaret of the deceived. Fragments of hate brewed from the tea leaves of brotherhoods forgotten family ties rend lives into the abyss. Hope in life fragments of blood droplets sprinkled on crimson clothing made snow white. The fragments of life droplets shed for all who choose wisely are the one true answer to death.

Froward

Self-willed manipulations orchestrate a racket into the harmony of the universe.

Recusant decisions jack-hammer life's mortar and hearts collapse in prosaic-verse.

Wayward elopers slide down ladders of deceit and land on hedges of provocation.

Obstinate hangers-on cling to rafts of inequity until they are capsized in liquation.

Dissentient groomers comb through strands of materialism increasing ignorance.

Willful used-car dealers negotiate envy and make odious deals with malevolence.

Ornery pig-headed dissident ministers drive their flocks into catacombs of trickery.

Contrary poker dealers skim the deck of parity to tip the scales to amoral bribery.

Unruly party planners negotiate caterers of avarice to indulge Pandora's dance.

Balky mules of illicit transactions litter the way of iniquity with appeal's chance.

Recalcitrant malefactors lure the unwary into acts of treachery to subdue candor.

Headstrong caretakers whip the meek pupils into mental states of despairing anger.

Perverse professors delude the unwise with false wisdom claims and outright lies. Contumacious financial advisors solicit wealth from the coffers of sordid buys.

Rebellious stewards construct layers of perplexity to rob their masters' vineyards.

Inverse ballet sponsors sway the thinking of children into mind numbing leotards. Disobedient fathers squander precious time and the suffering of their young grows.

Froward tongues lash young minds with words of fire that build embers' glows.

Frowsy

Slatternly distracted easily sway

in wafts of shame, we frolic where we may.

Remiss in duties wander away into armed cuties,

time crafts bars of steel into fabric most fey.

Negligent of time caps crumble to ash

piles of uselessness driven before wind crash.

Lax in watch butterfly chase a dream to botch

backs to truth eyes dazzled with sparkle trash.

Slack tasks thrown by to gutter glob stain

on robes not white riddled with self-pain.

Neglectful charge lost to rebirth high cost

foretell writ bindings of corpus gain.

Frowsy in deed toward waifs of rich harms

alley tripe's crumbs dropped in vain salt charms.

Sordid brands mark child's opal skin purity stark

give testimony to abuses by mind sharks.

Fugacity

Opportunity is squandered with a devout fugacity and we ignore a sound parable.

With winks and nudges we construct unstable towers of futility most contemptible.

Our time of choice is fleeting at best and passes quickly beyond a closed gate.

Pardon is briefly proffered; accept God's gift or reject truth and fall into an ill fate.

The cloak of deceit is donned to temporally hide from men inequity's vivid stain.

The light of hope's passing flame shines a beacon of righteousness to ease our pain.

A heavy price was paid by Christ and His ephemeral invitation is extended to all.

Kept from grace by our own decision we blame God for our exclusion and fall.

Broken as the brambles of segregation we ostracize the humble in pragmatic fervor.

Shafts of flitting opportunity shoot down from the canopy of ancient oaks of armor.

On a passing whim we net butterflies of inglorious pride for our own false glories.

Kneeling at the throne of judgment we weave webs of transparent mad sham stories. Unuttered, locked in throats of recognized guilt all lies are exposed to light's fire.
The grand jury of saints has now met and indicted the wicked who will expire.

Short-lived earthly riches are currently consumed by the moth and flame at eon's end.

Man's transitory training is finished and the alumnae of Love in eternity time spend.

Gambol

A leap of faith drops the shackles of bondage to sin and joy springs forth adoration. Containment of ecstasy is impossible and the pardoned's feet caper in conjunction. Doubts fall away from the ids of the amnesty receivers who frolic with seraphim. Childish glee abounds among the reprieved who cavort in life free from requiem. Un-tethered legs leap forth in dances of uncontained worship of the Grace Giver. The chains of oppression once released fall away forever and the liberated roister. Symbols' sweet notes resonate in the hearts of the forgiven and they bound into life. The prison doors flung wide by accepted grace, the released revel for lack of strife. Melodies of the flute of eternal exculpation rollick in the ears of absolved sinners. Lifelong slaves to indulgence, when freed, blink in awe but soon frisk as winners. Joyous praise songs shake the rafters from the throats of the exonerated who romp. The lambs of the slain Shepherd gambol beside still waters and on green grass chomp.

Garner

The briars proliferate and overtake the wheat which becomes choked and dying. The Light is now blocked and can no longer nurture the vine, which is soon crying. Master gardeners must continually cultivate the crops to remove carnality.

The plants support weeds in symbiotic toxic intertwining leading to death's finality. The gatherer's encouragement must be continuously provided from hands of love.

Weeding, pruning, plucking, watering are supplied by the Master's hand above.

A crop left untended soon withers under the heat of the sun and the harvest is lean.

The scythe has been sharpened to a fine edge and now is the time to cut and glean. Many seeds have fallen upon barren rock and have dried up in the heat and weep. The bounty is diminished as the blades of the combine thrash with little or no reap. Assessors tromp through the fields the gain to census, baskets of increase to inspect. The Grim Reaper stands ready at the margin of time awaiting empty souls to collect. The voice of treason oozes hate stifling seductions that suffocate in oil-glaze slather. The deft fingers of aides pluck single tufts as the grains of wheat they toil to gather. The war of renewal awakens the hope of faith to sing psalms at unjustified inquests. The correcting spreader of enrichment works to assure the way of plentiful harvests. Put down the hoes of correction, the spades of rectification and release the burner. Ripening time is now past and the seeds of grace are dispersed and ready to garner.

Gehenna

Barathrum awaits the brash carnal peddler
seduced into sin by the fallen meddler.
The stone gate of Sheol meets those of ill fate.
Tophet is the mulct for the wheedler.
Blazes stuffs unbelief into an eternal cage
of separation from a loving Father's sage.
The flames of Hell scorch the souls of shames
committed in the name of selfish rage.
Hades binds the slovenly into hot iron fetters
of everlasting reminders of choice getters.
The smoke of Perdition rises forever to choke
the unwitting hunters of jetsetters.
Gehenna rewards the idle with pretty trifles baubles
that strangle the unaware with lotus cobbles.
The Abyss's maw gapes for the feet of the raw
whose ignorance tumbles them in death wobbles.

Gloaming

The midday of our revelry is passed and the afternoon of our sorrows approaches.

The construction of our demise is designed and the building of deceit encroaches.

The foundations of our debauchery are laid upon the quicksand of wicked intent.

Dusk is imminent and the shadows stretch out their arms to gather knees unbent.

The late evening sun filters through the bare limbs of winter offering dim radiance.

The fifth hour is but a memory of hope on the distant horizon as pride is defiance.

The troops of malcontent march steadily, floundering in endeavors of soul misery.

Night falls on respecters-of-person who are windowless upon the depths of usury.

The hope of foolishness is placed in the strength of decaying corpses who haunt.

The champions of the unwise are the brothers of pomp and circumstance who jaunt.

The fortresses of the misled are constructed from the mists of pride, and prejudice.

Owl-light is trapping the unwary in acts of depravity that are caught incredulous.

The wisdom of the deceived is bound up in the science of flat earth glad delusions.

The theorem followers bind themselves together in serendipity argument infusions.

The lemmings make a mad dash for the goal at the seventh hour of a sea-foam end.

Twilight's last twinkle is falling away and the stars of loss dance in a blazing wind.

The ninth hour bell tolls a mournful peeling against the unprepared maidens' lamps.

The wicks are trimmed and extra oil hoarded by the maidens prepared as champs.

The unawares' flames smoldered and are out at the eleventh hour for lack of oil.

Darkness is consuming the last vestiges of light fleeing the earth's man-made toil.

The cankers of the betrothed to carnal brides' fester into the night and await trial.

The nod winkers smirk for the misled souls' debate as the gut releases acid bile.

The murderers of watchfulness wander the alleys of hate in iron shackles bound.

Eventide washes over the bone littered shores of the ignorant that night drowned.

The hands of fate are locking fingers with immoral flatterers who are unbelievable.

The second hand is past the twelfth hour and all choices are long past irretrievable.

The time of contrition is ticking away as the sham sands seep into Hell's sway.

Gloaming minutes are best used for supplication, zeal and Christ sharing display.

Glorification

A crown of grace awaits those who pursue Love with reverent humble loyalty. Apotheosis opens the gateway to the straight and narrow path leading to royalty. Ennoblement spreads before the feet of the lowly of spirit as they bow in trust. Robes of white drape the shoulders of the apostles in quintessence of life's dust. The basest servant shall reach the pinnacle of elevation upon surrendering authority. Exaltation is only achieved through meek unfaltering pursuit of faith into probity. The acme crumbles and the lowest gorge is lifted high unto dignification of soul. Immortalization twinkles in everyone's desire but only the broken are made whole. The post-mortem triumph awards are reserved for the steadfast Christ adherent. Ultimate mansions of splendor await the transition of the grace wrapped reverent. Bodies born of spirit await the glorification from the decaying to the everlasting. Deification has been bestowed upon the first reborn from death's sacrifice wasting.

Goaded

Compelled to do the first works and disseminate the good news to the ignorant, driven to step forth in faith and risk death at the hands of those devoid of real love, urged by the whispers of the Omnipotent to love even those who murder innocence, spurred on by a desire for all to come to the truth and live free and ridicule abounds, coaxed by the prompting of the Holy Spirit and to turn to truth ears opened hear, pricked by consciousness's response and convicted of inadequate blind stumbling, cajoled by truth's inalienable solidarity and bound together with all witnesses' faith, blandished by images of real life and hints of paradise found under a stained cross, prodded to bear witness to the corrupt souls and the lost wonderers of hopelessness, incited by the desires that none should fall short of the acceptance of the free gift, prompted by Love to cast fishing nets into the darkness hopeful of a good catch, propelled by unwilling feet and marched forward into the silent struggle with hate, goaded by the heart's convictions and upheld by the strength of self-weakness, exhorted by the Living Word embedded in hearts willing to be opened unto hate and the carrying out of the design by the Holy Spirit into the grace of the living God, we walk the straight and narrow path toward paradise of life given to those who ask, seek and with zeal pursue the truths of God's design through to the end of strife.

Grievous

The hands of life weave rugs of shame to hide children of opulent self-pleasure. Mouths of social morons spill words of deception over air-waves of ill-measure. Bitter rancid coffee ground dregs of government mandates wither work ethics. Onerous laws form ponderous chain lengths binding the working to a failing matrix. The arrogance, of the elected elite, forges bars of separation to imprison society. Oath-takers interpret laws to glue party lines into kaleidoscope LSD trips of piety. The mass hysterical cartwheel down the blood bowl parades to tunes of lies' rifts.

Deplorable socialistic tyranny elves hammer nails into the wrists of ignorance gifts.

Law-givers are locked behind closed doors to hammer deals with mammon pacts. Feet, of the waywardly inclined, rally under swindlers' poker tables offering racks. Acrid smoke wisp thermals rise over hate furnaces lined with the innocents' bones. Exigent participles are expounded from between the teeth of tossers of hard stones. The mournful cry out in abjection for lack of intersession into quagmires of idiocy. Deal-makers lay burdensome loads across the stooped shoulders of ailing duplicity. Hands, of the pat winkers, deal cards of decadence from the bed of marked decks. Weighty matters dangle perilously high on bribery tongued hot-air balloon wrecks. The demanding shout lash phrases against the middleclass supporters of candor. Wheel-greasers slather oils of affluence over squeaky money launderers of rancor. Arms, of the petulant, embrace the folds of gluttony to squeeze shares of plunder. Exacting tests of loyalty are administered by the sword to the hoards that blunder. The sorrowful lament their hardships encountered within the prison walls they erect. Bed-warmers of acceptance wallow in contractually bound agreements they select. Eyes, of solicitors, lock in judgmental stares onto the faces of the innocent who fear. Grievous wrongs are laid at the feet of hope and those guilty of hate shed not a tear.

Habituate

Exposed to venomous propaganda, continually, we are adjusted to accept wrong. Contact with the infected gives addiction to breeding sin viruses that grow strong. Subjected to false instruction we are conformed by accepting as truth many lies. Speech borne infectious hate conditions the senses of the weak knotting evil ties. Enslaved by the seamy adulterers we are devoted to our routines of hopelessness. Beauty bound eyes are immured to images of deliciously pleasing selfishness. Entrapped by silk strands of flattery we support orbs of indulgent illicit metaphors. Lips of seduction shape silent words of tolerance until death stalks the acceptors. Sickened by plagues of indulgence we are familiarized with malevolent intentions. Fingers of beckoning sign encouragements of conformation to occult inventions. Afflicted by rampant pandemic hardened hearts the needy are cast aside to die. Thighs of sexual perversions are seasoned with many liaisons for which we vie. Succumbed to widespread conformity we are shaped into acting puppets of Lucifer. Feet of clay swiftly flee to habituated opium houses of regurgitated riches juicier.

Hapless

Flock to mediums, tarot readers and soothsayers woefully we declare fate our lot. Religious adherence to astrological signs and wonders direly we sit and smoke pot. Devout attendees to spiritualism's cataclysmic services we bow to deceit's throne. Dance with harlots our calamitous choices bind us to the shackles of the ill-prone. Gather with the drifting, tragically we walk into a mirage of lush iridescent oasis. Herd mentality dictates our actions, disastrous consequences seize the ostentatious. Anthill antics link scholastic morons into baleful chain gangs of all-inclusiveness. Packs of irony glue pacts of the infelicitous into contracts of hardened intrusiveness. Conclaves of likeminded intertwine wretched slats of subversion binding the weak. Pods of sarcastic winkers sway the simpletons into miserable speeches of ill-speak. Gatherings of accusers throw spears of infelicitous condemnation at the naive. Gaggles, of euphemism honkers, sing catastrophic opera chorales on Allhallows eve. Assemblies of respecters-of-persons cast stones of malefic death-wishes at hope. Throngs of rioters push over the Phantoms of grim mammon bowers of gift dope. Congregations of religious proclamations add harsh weights to the pardon-broken. Choices not hapless fate spread the asphalt on freedom's highway by Christ-token.

Hedonism

Enamored with ourselves we consume life through egotistical satisfaction pursuits. Pleasure mongers all; we peddle drugged highs, deadly vices, and children's lives. Carnal hounds sniff out and devour purity, faith, hope and love in death's stench. Sybarites roam the land, roar as ravenous lions and rend the timid into submission. Onanistics chase illusions of joy down alleys filled with rats and offal of despair. Bon vivant dances in the blood of the slain for avarice and hate pleasure's fate. Voluptuary cavorts with the fallen angel of light to worship sin in their darkness. Epicure waltzes on the bones of the poor to melody cries of the oppressed poor. Sensualist world-minded workaholics pound out time in glass prisons of prosperity. Gourmand dabblers are swallowed in cesspools of rosy defecations of likeminded. Rakish swindlers con the masses with messages of tolerance slippages that enslave. Debauchee revelers wax fat on the sweat and blood of middleclass unapprised bees. Hedonism is the pandemic of the age stripping away the last shreds of humanity.

Honeysuckle Sweet

The honeybee sting of first love is bittersweet and strikes at the most inopportune moments in a young heart. Eleven, twelve, thirteen the vortex of bliss swirls round fogging the vision of blossoming youth. Middle school, high school beginnings of transition fashion hearts into cupped hands of gentle caresses as the fragile petals of honeysuckle vine hints of sweetness on a gentle breeze mid-summer. Dancing fireflies in May herald the oncoming rush of new found enchantments eager to be clasped to bosoms of pounding hearts and dry tongued hesitancy. Vacant expressions of remorse for past harsh words of teasing offer deceased apologies to the objects of unrequited affection. Fractured time skips across days of mundane circumstance so that an age without meaning stands between the unattainable goals of idol swooning as teachers' lofty ideals are attempting penetration of thick-skulled adolescents' preoccupation with the pigtails at the next desk over. Giggled whispers pound the ducked heads of lads giving sidelong glances at the objects of perseverant affections misplaced by seemingly unrelenting empty bellies laughs at first attempts of chivalry. The moon dances out of reach of all but the most obstinate or foolhardy dreamers of a neither goal. Starlight beckons weave patterns across vacuums trolling for tiptoes of solid footed realists who patiently chip away at life's barriers to obtain the closest semblance of greatness at the end of an arduous climb. Flakes of intolerance chipped from granite bigotries fly in all directions wounding indiscriminately all who are too close to the fear mongers' hammers. Grace weavers throw blankets of inclusion across the shoulders of the misfits to further love's lofty goal of self-respect for all persons regardless of demeanor, shape, gender, skin color, ethnic background, or any other perceived difference. Linked arms of solidarity form a chain far stronger than stone to which the willing bind themselves to propagate the freedoms across boundaries to include all of mankind. These acts of kindness when often repeated bring nations to the table of feasts to share the cornucopia of joys discovered. The first grains of wisdom start at the age of discovery and are multiplied as they become glued with love until a united freedom crosses out all differences pulling everyone into the infectiousness of brotherhood enticed by the sweet aroma of the honeysuckles of hope.

Hoppy

Hoppy is happy this sunny day of rest.

Night spent in feast with summer's bounty they are blest.

Long tails have hopped through the night long.

Little ears heard the owl's wing rustling in death's song.

Scattered in less than half a heart's beat, revelry fled.

To hesitate is to be caught for the Owl's feast torn and bled.

Hoppy is young and quick, his mother taught him well.

He's the first under the log at the Owl shadow's death knell.

The others have fled swiftly night death missed its mark.

Scattered in fear seeds left on leaf platters exposed, stark.

Little legs are thumping in the night summer's heat.

Owl soars with empty talon to a far limb retreat.

Seed orgy paused as heads are counted none lost.

The owl's frustration is joyous occasion without cost.

The break of sunlight burns the last shadows away.

Little bodies jump to the feast leaves sway.

Seeds gathered in to store for the next feast.

Summer's bounty will fatten the smallest, very least.

The mountain jumping mice's party is over.

It has been spoiled by the Owl's wild herding drover.

Hosanna

To the One who gives us breath, we cry up in supplication requests innumerable. Anguished souls look to worldly endeavors to ease their longings for fulfillment. For the One who sees when we are awake, we extol in praises of hope and faith. Carnally minded atheists deny myriads of truths for fear of understanding true love. On behalf of the One who watches while we sleep, we celebrate peace and comfort. Hordes of science worshipers dip swords of opulence into the blood of Redemption. Because of the unwavering of the One who discerns hearts, we glorify his Word. Untold minions of theory-swallowers spread lies from the pupils of the Dark Ages. Owing to the patience of the One who sees when we are good or bad, we laud Him. Worldly stricken blind pursuers wonder in darkness because of their stubbornness. Due to the One who gathers His sheep, we apotheosize His name without ceasing. Straying sheep flee toward seeming greener pastures that once consumed sicken. Thanks be to the One who truly loves unconditionally, we sing psalms of gratitude.

Lost lambs bleat helplessly among the thorns that trap them in circles of pretense. As a result of the One who pardons transgressions, we magnify his many blessings. Grief-stricken transgressors refute the offer of pardon because of their guilt denials. In response to the One who washes the feet of the repentant, we proclaim His glory. Reluctant flesh enslaved Satan tripe is hidden in every word and image that betrays. In recognition of the One who reprimands the wayward, we panegyrize His name. Millions upon millions of those who tread blindly down the broad path rebut truth. For the honor of the One who gives choices, we offer resounding hymns of worship. Sheep answering to the wrong master soon discover a ravenous wolf at their throats. For the joy in our Deliverer, Life-giver, and Love sharer, the humble shout hosanna.

Hound

The natural man has been harried into contortions of torment glee. Pursuits, of the baited, wind down dark alleys of greed at a high fee. The disciples of dust rise to persecute the spiritually minded steadfast. Endeavors, of the misled, vex death vultures over a putrid breakfast. The students of Id embrace themselves in hector hugs against belief. Deeds, of the deceived, mark words that bedevil the faithful's relief. The apprentices of treachery shoot false arrows that badger the truth. Accomplishments, of the duped, are as seeds sown in soil of no proof. The followers of mammon bully the poor into usurious serf pacts. Undertakings, of the lost, produce heavy burdens to chivy the facts. The cohorts of pride push around the meek making way for theft. Goals, of the opulent, harass the resolute until they have nothing left. The frat kings haze the recruits into acts of attrition till they crumble. Aspirations, of the world, hound the redeemed to make them stumble.

Humble

Clasp truth in your heart and be humble,

chase not the world for you will stumble.

To rally in the army of faith is to sally

forth in obedience and not bumble.

Bowed head and open arms of the lowly,

build great rewards of faithfulness slowly.

Answer the call to act and never turn back,

to ways once corrupt and apt solely.

Sew on the steel banner of the meek,

to repel the advance by the hate speak.

Slip in the corral's open gate assure safe fate,

and join the Master's sheep whom they seek.

Bent knees, bared heart of the inert,

strengthen the arms of the permissive.

Don the white smock of the Shepherd's loyal flock,

and life will be most comprehensive.

Hypocrisy

Cant swirls the smoke of falsehoods around shadowed blurred faces. Pecksniffery slips on the cloak of conceit hiding malicious op laces. Pharisaism builds opaque glass veneers over sooty mark flue cracks. Tartuffery slips easily into thick fog trousers of misdirection slacks. Pietism paints over the mordent façade of carnality to hide hungers. Casuistry veils the archaic sophistry within purple cloth mongers. Sham masks are donned by hoodwinkers stirring cauldron potions. Charlatanry skips among the Mardi Gras masks of off-glib notions. Sanctimoniousness flaunts golden cufflinks that bind id slaves. Unctuousness banters words of ill omen into bard song conclaves. Glibness composes knife concertos that slice the faces of sincerities.

Hypocrisy bands together the iniquitous into mobs of jolly duplicities.

I am Young

My age is a number without a voice.

I grow older by years but not by choice.

At nine, hop scotch and marbles was the find.

At ninety-nine they play over in my mind.

At fifteen a dance was so cool.

When seventy-five, they think me an old fool.

Turned twenty-one and a new spouse I was to be.

Then eighty and a look, beside me a twenty-year-old I still see.

Forty came quickly down upon me just as a song.

Middle age they said would last so long.

Yesterday I was forty today one hundred three.

Oh, so I wish to be forty again and so free.

Time is so swift, passing in a blink.

To the Doc's office I go, look at all the old people, I think.

My age is a number without meaning or time.

In my dream I still play hopscotch and marbles as if I were nine.

One hundred twenty goes as quickly as five.

Though my body is old, my mind is still youthfully alive.

Identic

Equivalent, balanced, blended the Father and the Christ are one. Indistinguishable in deed and in love the perfect will is being done. Tantamount wills, spoken Word do harmonious concordance deeds. Exact images reflected actions, build realms of spirit woven seeds. Duplicate natures instruct solidarity lessons into open ears of acumen. Identical compassions pass over the faults to contrite hearts amend. Equal in gift offers grace abounds to those who ask in steadfast belief. Identic, as one they orchestrate a balance of time and sins' pain relief.

Idyll

The snowbirds herald the weather change midwinter's solstice. Chickadees hearken at the windowpane for rattling seed poultice. Kingfishers glide the serpentine creeks for open water berths' scale. Jays jostle the back deck cat food bins for dominate post no avail. Cardinals flit through last year's Hosta-pods for small kernel bits. Wrens whisper softly through sheds' open doors for warm sits. Titmice tap glass portholes of questions seeking perchance consent. Pastoral silent moving picture shows in Technicolor ply advent. Agrestic portraits of simplistic beauties are framed in ardent blues. Campestral watercolors softly reflect the winter sun's spectra hues. Provincial harmonies of stream gurgles and wind chimes sing joys. Compliant contentment bounces on exuberant legs of country boys. Rustic charms soften big city harms from reluctant work pressures. Beautiful episodes of baby sheep ballets dance in flowers' gestures. Bucolic carpets of yellow daisies give soft hued frolic arenas essence. Rural simplicities ease anxieties in nature's spa retreats of presence. Natural balm oils flow in raindrops through pine needle umbrellas. Idyll dance moves erase memories of concrete car fume hack-nebulas.

Immaculate

An unblemished Rose of Sharon shines among the brambles of hate. A perfect diamond sparkles out of the mud coated swine of ill fate. Virtuous humble servitude instructs the ignorant in acts of kindness. A flawless ship sails over seas of ignoble deeds to remove blindness. An impeccable character accepts the horrid burdens of the doomed. An undefiled heart of love reprieves the souls of the entombed. Righteous obedience opens barred gates and gives access to the lost. A faultless sacrifice makes payment for the guilty unmindful of cost. A pure soul transcends the tomb of death to shine light on truth's way. Of clean garments in pure white shine down guiding those who stray. Spotless service gives testimony to God's grace without complaint. An immaculate birth, a life without sin the Living Word does not faint.

Imp

Whispered enticements float in the shadows cast by inglorious imposters. Words of deceit suggest acts of immorality to those without armor. Hints of rebellion tickle the ears of those who listen for rationalizations. Allusions of opulence sparkle before the eyes of the misled. Propositions of transgressions bombard the wavering brides of sedition. Offers of surfeit flood the desires of the rapacious with inducement. Deals of subversion are laid on the tables of the treacherous with clauses of duplicity. Pacts of dissension are orchestrated by musicians of cacophony in melodies of discord. Treaties of the impious are signed by the invisible pens of malice. Settlements of decreed divorce are married with betrayal in the darkness. Citations of quoted euphemisms are uttered to placate the immoral sensitivity of bias transgressors. Extracts of vanilla are sprinkled on the putrid debauchery of the corrupt to hide their stench. Rumors of wrongdoing are attributed to the innocent to subvert the truth into subjugation. Anecdotes of false witnesses are uttered at the trials of the faithful to condemn fidelity. Chronicles of mendacity are recorded in the journals of the con artists to swindle the uninformed. Records of reproof are filed in the cabinets of the judgmental to incriminate the wrongfully accused. Voices of attrition erode the stones of complacency and the lukewarm are spewed through the cracks. Counsels of imps are broadcast bombarding the bastions of hope with missiles of discouragement. Sneers of demons are cloaked behind the hordes of blinded.

Imperious

Blind goats trudge willingly behind blind goats driven by greed. Goaded ever onward by the heavy hand of the one who deceives. Laughing as though free to do as we will yet servitude is indeed. Forced along paths of pain and arbitrary suffering no one perceives. Joyously driven by a whip of choices we mock ourselves in lies. Mandated servitude laid down on willing necks is a tedious weight. Gladly chained into gangs of rebellion oppressive revelry cuts ties. Forced bondage by a swindler counterfeits we trudge into hate. Sparkling diamond auroras dazzle the sight of obsequious opulent. Controlled by desires' manifestations we congratulate a tipped scale. Smooth waters ripple falsehoods we dive in cesspit's toxic flocculent. Mastered by many delving desires we cuddle our captor's death pail. Hypnotized by ticking gold coins we reap rewards of the iron caged. Subdued by hands offering fools' gold wealth we jump into a hot pit. Conned by eagerness to pleasures we plod into mobs of the enraged. Absolute possession welcomed trap taken riches that will never fit. Seduced with nectar liquors, power drunkards wallow in vomit pride. Stringent adherence to loose morals sways the unwitting into ill acts. Pied Piper melodies lure the unprotected into swirling illusion's side. Imperious curses flow freely from Lucifer's lips binding the ones lax.

Infirm

In weakness strength is allotted through faith and perseverant works. Of fragile might edifies humility and leads to reliant fellowship perks. Powerless submission builds vigor of purpose making the small great. The feeble bodies of the wizened bring low the haughty in stolid fate. A spindly frame builds mighty caucuses of belief under the cross. Insubstantial flesh holds vessels of pure hearts that bind up all loss. Enfeebled feet carry the weary into martyrdom as their voices plead. Puny arms hold up babes of devotion and are made burly in deed. Sickly bodies give birth to humble spirits that influence moral change. An impuissant, thorn in the flesh refines the soul into a capable range. The unfit are honed by Love to transcend weaknesses for prominence. The infirm hand wields the mightiest sword of peace in dominance.

Innervate

We ask why disasters oft arise,

and the honest answer is no surprise.

Once we slap God's face we begin an evil race;

kindle fires of wrath at each new sun's rise.

Wicked acts incense the flame that chides

till the hand that guards no longer abides,

seditious minds that close to love's healing vines.

Incite riots and wonder death on all sides.

We provoke the One that gives our rest

over and over we run Him through the test.

Just anger wields a rod that turns feet to fields

full of peace, hope and love's bountiful best.

Lies portend the rod's purpose scoffed, run

and scurry we flee truth and we are never done

with immoral deed and of coals the fires feed,

till sins innervate and will Armageddon's Son.

Irradiate

The call of God beseeches a willing hand to open the door to light. Footsteps down the path to edification begin with a response to love. Hardship is encountered to refine the spirit's trust in the Lord of hosts. The Living Word instructs the ready soul in matters that mature it. Evil is allowed reign to kindle the fires of passion of spiritual truth. Without experiencing dark, enlightenment holds a diminished luster. Instruction to the wise falls on open ears and illumes the spirit. Faithful disciples strive toward perfect service working over failures. Once ignited, the flame of service burns through the dark to uplift. Faith responds to Love and fulfills peace, hope and joy of exaltation. Overcome fears illuminate true followers and their candles are bright. Standing firm to the end polishes the heart to a brilliant radiance. Once redeemed, good deeds highlight the faithful and glorify God. Darkness, when acknowledge and turned from, uncovers brightness. Steadfast study of that which is Holy makes for a refined finish. Achieve your purpose by irradiation with Christ's redemption offer.

Jade

The hand of deceit weaves robes of delusion that oppress the unwary. The feet of waywardness carry the iniquitous till they are satiated. The plate of gluttony is heaped with opulence that gluts the simple. The wealth of the greedy lays on their shoulders a weight that crushes. The hand of the unsatisfied reaches out for more until it finally tires. The fires of the workaholics send up a pall of choking wasted time. The ever-hungry grope about eating to excess, but never get their fill. The dead, who walk, give rise to a cloying stench polluting the fickle. The incessant lies of the duped grow noses that unerve the reckless. The nefarious build power bastion realms of surfeit to dazzle the poor. The spiritually starved gorge themselves on the offal of the idolatrous. The voices of persuasion jade the morally frail with swirling chimera.

Join

Total freedom is achieved when we bind to the Grace Giver's hem. United with truth, discernment illuminates the treachery of a whim. True peace blankets the shoulders of the Christ-fused who stand firm. Melded flesh and spirit alloy, the graced are guarded by a faith berm. Hope fills those who merge with the Holy Spirit's guiding whispers. Connect with the only true love who teaches patience during vespers. Joy radiates from the faces of the ones coupled to the Engine of Life. Affixed to the sleeve of the Intercessor we are lifted above all strife. Love knits the wounds of those who open their doors to His knock. Married to the Prince of Peace the freed are wary of those who mock. Faithfulness links the contrite heart to the chain of a full life's joy. Coalesced in the armies of the Living God disciples truth employ. Pierced hands reach out to join the called to God's spiritual war. Amalgamate with Christ before it is too late for death is at the door.

Journey

A faith walk is a lifelong peregrination first in flesh last in spirit. Many choices are set in doors at every side of the trek of the hopeful. Those stuck in the flesh sample every door till disorder mars the trip. The steadfast keep their eye on the spirit that guides their voyage. Wayward feet find paths of destruction on which they sally forth. Wise discernment follows grace in pilgrimages of unwavering hope. The nefarious travel off road into thickets of self-imposed burdens. The meek stay with the sacrificial expedition of truth unto eternal life. The deceived take side excursions with flesh dabblers that murder. The freed remain with the tour by choice to experience all fullness. World minded make many jaunts to fulfill the lusts of their hearts. Forgiven faithful move with steady progress even when they slip. Flesh hungry readily jump ship to join cruises of decadent deception. The safari to capture life is led by the one who willingly gave his. Predetermined answers draw the loath to change on junkets of hate. Life's journey is only rewarded when the path of rectitude is taken.

Jubilant

Exultant expectation lifts the feet of belief from the ground of hate. Triumphal grace accepters are taken up with joy in their happy fate. Glad tidings are sung in wondrous melodies of hope through belief. Thrilled participants with open heart doors find the ultimate relief. Joyous renditions of highest praises rise up on voices of the absolved. Elated feet dance on golden streets with unconditional love resolved. Delighting hands weave cords of faith to throw down to the craven. Rejoicing arms uplift in worshipful thanks for the salvation driven. Euphoric faces shine with the light of redemption as they ascend. Happy reunions meet in the skies of kinship on Christ they depend. Ecstatic reprieved stand firm in thanksgiving with Hosannas sing. Jubilant overcomers drink of the river of life and praises to God bring.

Judicious

A discerning ear recognizes false doctrine and evades deadly snares. A knowing heart follows truth onto paths of righteousness and cares. An astute mind conquers ignorance until truth burns brightly in hope. A shrewd intellect holds up the candle of faith that burns hate's rope. A wise choice turns many feet toward the path to eternal life's spring. An insightful decision opens doors of opportunity and joy bells ring. A perceptive eye sees past the veil of pretense to the hands of deceit. A sagacious understanding builds bridges of unity that defeat conceit. An intuitive curiosity cuts paths in stone purposes for the love graced. A perspicacious humble heart walks with humility and is peace laced. A Gnostic decider stalwartly struggles over thorns of evil briberies. An acute understanding is sharpened by the word and severs rivalries. A cogitative person reviews ostensible truths with the words of Christ. A judicious understanding corrects the ignorant in love that is spliced.

Just

Convicted, we deserve the maximum sentence.

A proper and contrite heart gives penance.

Fitting wages we earn by choices made in wrong rages.

Merited penalty is a heavy weight of immanence.

Chained in suitable bonds, the guilty meet fates.

A rightful verdict is handed down, hunger never satiates.

Rhadamanthine rulings obtain copious justice in pain.

True judgment flows from the One invigorates.

Damned, we deny the requisite words of hope.

A repentant mind depends on grace not dope.

Right decrees mete sound penalties at defeat.

Due measure burdens the wicked refusing to cope.

Pardoned are those who on the Redeemer wait.

A trustworthy advocate seals souls whose fears abate.

Amnesty is set to whom the book is fete.

Just words spill from lips pleading past the gate.

Juxtaposed

Come near to the Grace Giver and find peace beyond comprehension. Stand beside the Pierced Hands and join the fold of a life everlasting. Become linked in the Spirit and obtain help onto the path of rectitude. Build your house on the rock adjacent to the Foundation Stone of life. Tend your contiguous garden with seeds of enlightenment to the lost. Stand touching the open side of the Redeemer until the battle is won. Be a good neighbor with an open door of invitation to the ignorant. Walk in the Shepherd's flock, conterminous harmony a light of hope. Be planted as a cedar of Lebanon, juxtaposed to the kingdom of God.

Kernel

A crux of gold bound in a torn and pierced shell rewards the absolved. The center of purity is enshrouded with humbleness staying involved. An essence of life exudes from the breath of the King giving all hope. The Sum of ages trod a rabbi's path that led to death's slippery slope. A heart of love beats in the bosom of Redemption calling all within. The thrust of the Word is aimed at all minds for instruction to begin. A foundation laid on the Cornerstone of eternity will never fracture. The tenor of faith ties the willing to the scarred hands holding rapture. A purport is laid on the souls of those who accept the free grace gift. The core of belief weaves a thread of brotherhood repairing the rift. An upshot of opening to the knock of opportunity is everlasting joys. The Gist of salvation is the open arms of unconditional love's ploys. The strength of grace is unbreakable only by embracing truth to heart. A kernel of love may grow to infinity if fed from God's Manna cart.

Keystone

The Apogee of faith may be achieved by living in humble devotion. The Source of all love must be welcomed inside with bared emotion. The Culmination of hope has the ear of Omnipotence in intercession. The Capstone of grace spreads arms of acceptance thru confession. The Acme of reawakening bought our lives with heartache and pain. The Support for our frailty walks beside the faithful who do not wane. The Crest of peace carries the surfers of steadfastness into a calm sea. The Pinnacle of glory holds the beacon that calls all from sin to flee. The Ultimate friend paves the road to glory with bricks of his blood. The Zenith of worship calls his sheep, which He saves from the flood. The Conqueror of death, crowned in victory, is the first man eternal. The Keystone of joy in the arch of Heaven gives life waters supernal.

Kindled

Inflamed with a passion to serve by our redemption we should shout. Fomented with the sparks of everlasting life we should share it about. Excited with the good news of grace we should proclaim it to all. Provoked by the blood of sanctification we become ushers to the ball. Roused with fervors for blessings we spill good acts onto humanity. Fired up about the love of God we flee the world's lusts and insanity. Blazing with intent to uplift the downhearted we give sustenance. Aroused to action we must give aid to the weary in our abundance. Incited to battle for lost souls we distribute the Word to the lost. Stirred by compassion we succor in empathy regardless of cost. Stimulated by unsurpassed peace we must offer a place to the weary. Lit by the match of salvation we are asked to assert truth to the leery. Flared into brilliance we shine our lights as a beacon to the last hope.

Knell

The clapper draws back to strike the first sound of the twelfth hour. Seconds flow swiftly toward the appointed time's first toll of the end. The hand has pulled the bell's rope and drawn the last hooray tower. The first peal is sounding and the wicked to their wills other bend. The mallet is arcing back to start the second gong and the dark bleeds. The moment's breath is held in anticipation of the chime's last edict. The second ring is reverberating with testimonies of man's evil deeds. The hammer is falling rapidly and the clang is to be heard in verdict. Time leaps in answer to the angels' loosening and their purpose nears. The third bong echoes around the globe and all hears its woeful voice. The strike-plate is cocked and the awakening stirs lost souls' fears. The hour of triumph is come and the clangors of faithful men rejoice. The fourth resounding bears witness to the fall and exposes all hopes. Arms swing for the fifth clash to announce the coming of a new age. The race's finish line draws near and with every signal malice mopes. The fifth knell bounces down empty streets as the cruel brood rage.

Knit

Fractures heal with time and when properly tended.

Relationships are united and with words mended.

Open hearts join souls separated who never departs.

Rifts are bridged by many kindnesses become blended.

Tears are reconnected by patient words worked.

Broken thoughts merge in hope when faith is not shirked.

Shattered pieces have a new bond in amended leases.

Wrongs may be put-right by those deemed quirked.

Unraveled threads are plaited by true lexis spoken.

Splintered lives are fused with a reconciliation token.

Leaks in peace veins are repaired by humbleness trains.

Snapped devotions are tied by love being woken.

Right instruction weaves a carpet of wisdom's choice.

Grace binds the repentant into life's hope voice.

Take God's bond repent and hold a grace wand.

Knit your spirit to Christ's and be God's joist.

Kvetch

Malcontents stir the vat of graciousness to blend in the rotten apples of disorder that spoil the entire batch. Wily deceivers play films of desire to initiate yawping among the weak minded. Blight is spread through subtle bellyaching from those who lust after their neighbor's ass. Petulant childish jealousy bleats out unceasing fussiness into the ears of the impatient who vacillate. Misdirected good intentions build murmurings between the workers and structure teeters. Serpents of id whisper hissed temptations into the midst of the wavering to instill yammering divisions of dissatisfaction. Neighborhood coveting erodes the foundations of opulent houses and soon the decay spreads darkness by mutterings in every direction. Birds of a feather throw hen parties, where they grouse against the good deeds of the humble. Click conclaves bolster egos with back pats and back-stabbing grumblings against the weaknesses of their peers. The unhappy lost bemoan their places in life and gripe against those who are content. Oft repeated phrases founded in kvetches slowly eat away the cliffs of granite that protect their stronghold against the never easing high-tide waves. Unwarranted complaints build into virulent glass-house shattering notes and the fractures spread throughout all nations.

Lament

Lament the war, for the lines have been drawn and sides are chosen. The ignorant amass behind death and damnation to their dire ruin. Great sorrow has landed on the minds of the deceived who see not. The lost take up the shout of death, death to the innocent ones. Anguished souls cry out petitions for those who choose great harm. Those strayed sheep run pell-mell into the rending fangs of reverie. Wailing and gnashing of teeth rise mournfully into death's smoke. The willful unaware cast spears of hate into the tearful eyes of faith. Weeping floods the hallways of the opulent with tears of love's loss. The goats, who wander aimlessly, chase lie wisps over the precipice. Grieved family members watch helplessly as egos claw loved ones. Obstinate children define success by their pairs of golden coffin nails. The bereaved rue the loss of the faithless that fall into a smoking pit. Biddable weak-willed listen intently to the falsehoods of the proud. Those who mourn the sin ensnared find comfort through grace's gift. The lemmings, in waiting, dance to desire's misleading and drown. The self-enslaved bemoan their plight putting blame on the pardoned. Dazzled moths flutter aimlessly into the flame of their destruction. Sing songs of sorrow, recite epic poems of mourning, orate speeches that bewail the loss of one hard-hearted soul, instruct the ignorant so that joy may be returned to the world.

Laughter

Laughter came down as a gift to the oppressed.

Laughter bursts forth at the slightest nudge.

Laughter is a free, given to those who need hope.

Laughter is the outward pouring of love's release.

Laughter is the hate purging reward of the blessed.

Laughter is the benefactor of good tidings of joy.

Laughter provides the endorphins of delight.

Laughter opens the gates of rejoicing.

Laughter shines in facets of rainbow lights twinkling in the crystals of life.

Laughter gives warmth to the cold hearts of the cynical.

Laughter opens doors for the spreading of love.

Laughter binds together the common knots of friendship with the glue of communication. Laughter melds the chemicals of attraction into one.

Laughter shares hopes and dreams of the fantasy driven.

Laughter swirls between the stars' dance.

Laughter tolls the final hour of the bell clapper's concordance in the book of instruction. Laughter peels past words of strife to the very heart of the elucidation.

Laughter grows inward to break the core of trepidation.

Laughter is as contagious as the dolphin's chirping tango.

Laughter gathers across heritages to darn the rifts of ignorance.

Laughter weaves handmade quilts of hope binding our differences.

Laughter gleans the particles of truth from a room full of lies.

Laughter seals the heinous' mouths with stitches of infectious bliss.

Laughter releases the shackles of slavery to wretchedness.

Laughter, you should let loose today and be free.

Laughter, you should embrace today and join the exclusive club of the freed.

Laughter ties all voices together in a chorus of infectious joy.

Laughter binds together all peoples across all ethnicity into shared love.

Legato

As sand grains through an hour glass our life moments fall away and are lost in the smog of routine. Smooth and even concertos lull our disassociations into compliance with Big Brother's dictations. As smoke wisps from fading embers, human heartbeats whisper sadly of forgotten freedoms. Dancing treble notes twirl amid thrumming bass vibrations and die in the silent alms. As starlight drops reflected in dawn's dew, we evaporate in hate's smelting ovens. Piping flute trills run amok at the bugle's wake-up blast that heralds unwanted change. As hummingbird wings blur above the flower's nectar, our eyes mislead into acts of unwitting stupidity. Trilling Chickadee melodies flare announcements of our helplessness to think independently and the herd mentality invades. As moonbeams in waterfalls' mists, we waiver at the changes in our short-term predicaments. Frolicking kids bleat out joyous songs of contentment in safe pastures ringed in razor-wire statutes. As eidolon hide among the tombstones at sunrise, light exposes the truth's relevance only when the candle remains lit. Chanting media whores pander decadence to the mulish defrauded who willingly slam the hammer on their own fingers. As illusionists misdirect attention from reality, lies mesmerize babes into sacrificial missteps. Falsetto harmonies attune the listener's ear to conveyances of deceit and lack of knowledge compounds our stumbling. As legato strings placate free thinking the wicked tighten the noose and we are choked by the lack of oxygen which speeds confusion. Death marchers beat the bass drum steadily drawing unknowing feet within eternity's furnace.

Lessor

Our Proprietor holds the key to the laundry room where transgressions' stains are removed. The Owner of the universe leases out His prized possessions to ungrateful husbandmen. Her benevolently Overseer showers gifts of grace on her shoulders of contrition. His light-handed Landlord provides a feathery yoke for his shoulders that work with easy burdens toward righteousness. The tenants' Super waits by the phone to address all failures with swift repairs, if called. The Master of the gate keeps a brighter light for the lost if only they turn to see. The Lessor of our living tabernacles extends a contract of hope to the faithful who are willing to sign their names in His book of life. We are boarders only and hold no title to anything we have. Tenants of our fleshly unit we abuse our charge. Occupants by permission we withhold payment of rent to our own undoing. Leaseholders in name we sign only the portion of the contract that we write. We have made slums of our duplexes through rents paid to fraudulent parties. Lessees of our souls we misuse the Superintendent's gift of free choices and enslave our birthrights.

Lichen

Feet weary from too much rest plod upward into chained sophistry. Shackled hands pull incessantly at willow-the-wisp deep lacerations. Last year's leaves crunch dryness under wayward footsteps' bruises. Weeping strings of hart's skin drip despondency onto moss spores. Freckled dimples remind the fence posts of calves' dehorned pains. Stiffened fingers struggle to grasp truth's lie steeling children's joy. Crumbled stones shed tears of sand onto the carpet of innocence lost. Splintered firs spread bowed limbs of sorrows over naked stone bone. Frozen slate spill white and blue waterfalls of stopped time in blood. Fronds of renewal unfurl as winter's snow ripples into tadpole pools. Tentative melodies reach cautiously for moonbeam trysts to revive. Whispered chemicals scream the pain of wars with unseen hoards. Granite embraces the lichen of testimony which renders them pebbles.

Lightening Bugs in June

Lightening bugs in June are a child's delight.

They flicker and glow brighter than the full moon's light.

Laughing hands snatch bugs from the dew laden grass blades.

Light pours between little fingers clasped tight in yellow beamed shades.

Puppy's tail is slapping across bare legs flapping, chasing dreams.

Giggles and summersaults over a yard full of children's joyous screams.

Happiness abounds when we are open to see it reflected in a child's eye.

Admonish from the porch shadows or become a child before we die.

The question is simple enough for anyone who wishes to see.

But the answer is elusive, hidden in plain sight the child's laughter holds the key.

Joy is most contagious if we but reach out and embrace it, frolic un-caged.

Money cannot buy it, power cannot force it, and children are wiser than the aged.

The lessons of life become our chains drawing tighter with time.

We bind our own shackles tighter and tighter choked we can no longer rhyme.

Turn around and look is all we need do to see clearly faithful joy.

Simplicity is lost when we look but do not see, mired either brazen or coy.

With each turn of the clock's hands, we burden our children into little adults.

Molded and shaped till all happiness is smothered in expectation of grown-up occults.

Best spend time with a child today, not in chagrin or impatiently tolerant they are in vain.

Limerick

Snowy verses float down fiery yellow furnaces of sapphire dreams.

Epic rhymes bleed across ten thousand pages of drivel, bruising toes.

Flute trills echo the dirge of helpless sailors caught in chaos throws.

Sousa's compositions march across fields to nuclear daisy die-deems.

Sonnets of Giacomo Da Lentini writ fourteen bars that illume edicts.

Knitters of elegies thread sound strands into needle eyed donkey sighs.

Quintessential feasts spread buttery odes of illusion onto burned fixes.

Crashed and flamed couplets discharge oozing bits into sound nixes.

Homer's heroic poems knit iron bars of slammed cell door finalities.

Multi-lingual stanzas bind broken dispersions into commonalities.

Silver threaded, beloved nursery rhymes open innocent eyes.

Requiem operas conduct final rights for the duly departed conductors.

Irish limericks dance on grass mounds of dead accordance's' first cries.

Liturgy

Steeped in tradition, man-made ritual thrives.

Ceremony supersedes truth and chance hate rives.

Ancient rites delude life's options and hopes preclude.

Well-meant observances cause corruption of lives.

Sacraments proffered with no love always fail.

Religious dogma blinds the convicted frail.

Impious creeds warp attempted well intended deeds.

Perverse doctrines twist minds putting prophets in jail.

Writs of belief shred the faithful's true witness.

Systematic repetitions undermine virtuous fitness.

Unholy canons erode weak faith's corridor code.

Profane services crack the vacillating salvation business.

Systems of belief, bound by Lucifer, fool mass.

A tenet of lies hides death's mask most crass.

Wrong precepts mash rotten apples spoiling the whole basket stash.

Liturgies of corruption accept lies vast.

Lugubrious

Eyes of ignorance stare dolefully from downcast faces into crowded happenstance. Wayward feet trod useless paths of meaningless pursuits on cheerless stone concourses leading to flights boarding onto criminality. Oppressive privateers hoard rusty treasures piled into warehouses of indifference mauling their neighbors. Anthill scurrying purposes build saturnine razor fences around poverty-stricken laborers in concentration camps of illicit demands. Depressed economies of scale abound from the pens of the morbidly obese government's soul pandering law auctioning freedom to the highest bidders. Heavy burdens of undermining self-determination termites destroy an empire's trustworthiness with somber ally interferences. Secret Santa terrorists give gifts of destruction to leaders greedy for power and influential poppycock while the poor languish in morose abjection from wonton deprivations. Gloom and doom nay-Sayers promote pessimism and burden hope with the weight of a million tons of helplessness. The children of task idolatry watch life pass them by through melancholy eyes programmed by media possession hype. Dour advice spills from the lips of the perpetually dissatisfied corrupting the easily swayed into treasonous slips-of-the-tongue. Jaws clinched in sullen obstinacy ignore truth at all costs to further ambiguous exclusion agendas. Countenances of iron glum glare at joy until it succumbs to hate's withered vine. A sad day dawns under a sun shrouded in the haze of lugubrious faithless mercy killer's inaction and death comes quietly to 6.9 billion un-reprieved.

Malice

Patiently chipping chinks in the armour of steadfastness, malice bends ignorance into a sharp two-edged sword slicing the wielder. Charming Venus Flytrap frills entice the discontented onto beds of pleasure sheets thinly covering despite's razorblades. Subterfuge glosses over the heavily bloodstained duvets as evil smiles from unassuming portrait's eyes. Spite sashays behind opulent window-pains in red-satin gowns thrilling the lusts of teenage stuck hounds caught unawares. Crypts of umbrage are draped in wisteria vines hiding death's nature under life's fragrant pillow. Grudge clingers-to pour concrete bastions around their miserable life essences hiding shame from all except their own minds. Rush hours of invidiousness trample the humble under iron feet madly dashing into insatiability. Flung birdseeds of maliciousness scatter onto the runways of newness lost upon preoccupied minds. Ink blotches dance across psychosis impaired MD's repertoire ammunition to bolster enmity against one's past and future selves. Crusty twice used bath water floats malevolence onto dippers who share the warm cradles of societal misconceptions. Incessant coveting expounds dissatisfaction until hate sprouts from free spending soils built under the feet of the broken-hearted. Ill-will ambassadors smile and wave while injecting contagions of animus into the minds and hearts of fawning dependent impressionable charges. Wickedness, wearing masks of normalcy, continually walks beside the naïve and the masses fully deceived smile and wink with total unawareness.

Marionette

Right pinkie dances, right leg prances in orchestrated mechanizations. Right thumb twitches, left leg ditches in reflexive knee jerk burlesque. Right index spins, left arm begins a thoracic conduction of weakness. Right ring tweaks, right arm speaks with silent implorations to face. Right obscene gestures, torso postures in provocative lewd exhibits. Left pinkie twirls, left leg swirls showcasing control's synchronicity. Left thumb bends, right knee sends signals of impulse jive responses. Left index jumps, right arm pumps in a salute of unwitting obedience. Left ring slides, left arm abides in subservient acts of harsh treachery. Left obscene rises, torso surprises shocked eyes with ill provocations. Marching in deluded independence our marionette strings play fiddle litanies as we are manipulated into death's doorways by the hands of our ever-present invisible puppeteer, Lucifer.

Metamorphosis

Spinning, spinning, ever spinning a cocoon of renewal life's lessons learned are by trial and error. Preschool to preteen is but a ballet of faith played upon the stages of things hoped cracked mirror. Upward sloping exclamations punctuate mistakes that fall by the way of beginnings understood. Rims of smoking experiments encircle the journeys' joys with temperance gifts sentinels stood. Enthusiasm knocks oft on young hearts' doors, but the knob had need to be turned from within. Fractured dreams fly on butterfly wings through missing window panes into renewed chagrin. Sandcastles soar heavenward between hands that practice finger dances into uncharted waters. Decay holds no quarter with sons' skills learned, and rotten fabrics of time are shed by daughters. Who once timidity held in bondage of carpeted imagination imprisonments are now flown free. Howbeit time has not yet paused for reflection on a short-lived endeavors' flowing water debris. Pupa for a second hand's fractured tick before the catalyst is stirred into life's sweet batter mixed. As to yeast in warm dough the rise comes quickly in a time of uncertain changes birth transfixed. Brightly colored toy balls yield to complex merging of teachers' words transform understanding. Scientific reasoning overbalances belief in all things unseen creating cracks in basis expanding. Crushes unfold in the newness of feelings unlearned but found by the wayside in unusual places. Hearts speed with abandonment toward goal posts shrouded in the mist of hoped for embraces. Connections are joined in rare mutual pacts of remote-controlled puppeteers' five finger dances.

Fascinations with new things embraced fades quickly under distractions' new wave chances. Transfigurations pop in random sequences as balloons under sharp darts flung in succession. Voices deepen, bosoms blossom, accidental whiskers sprout, between affairs off questions. Modification by rejection proliferates almost adults not yet but groping in the deep chasm. Searching a change to be had by perseverance toward goals of metamorphosis' new spasm.

Metronome

Clacking incessantly a mundane rhythm of helplessness, tied to the apron strings of redundancy, bound into subservience by ignorant choices, waiting on the table of cruelty and oppression while a small voice whispers encouraging hints of twinkling stars into the inky blackness of time metering, hoping to catch one ear of the lost five and a half billionth timid cricket scurrying in the dark, afraid of all light, hopelessly bound to countless other delusional morbidly obtuse lemmings rushing through life toward an untimely demise into a chasm of self-propulsion flung off the edge of reality, swallowed into white topped frothy waves of incredulously simple concordances of an overly spiced stew gone horribly wrong which gags the palate of the few remaining tastes of consequence seeking to bolster the failings of others with weak intrusions of paradigms lacking substance for the starving masses dithering in the storm drains of the opulent minority for scraps of wealth to cling wretchedly to while kicking their less fortunate neighbourhood bums in the ribs in order to discourage self-improvement actions that may contend with subliminal corporate ads lining the cone cells of eyes that refuse to see truth staring down the barrels of pride into reflections of children forgotten in scrambles to achieve the next ladder step toward stardom's successes of madness, addictions, and immoral cleaving to the razor wire shingles of the metronome of life's single purposed greed endeavours misguided fools abound.

Misprision

Bound into the river's lapping swirls, buoyant permission bobs along wistfully into treacherous waters. Released into iron shackles, rigid complacency ends without hopes of a future as duty dies on the poisoned vine. Transfixed with the spear-point of betrayal flamboyancy heralds lies with pomp and circumstance propaganda cupcake platters. Freed from obligations, contracted leashes entwine the translucent wavering decision-phobia driven synopsis avoiders of productivity. Riveted into buttery sticks of livid invitations, syrupy remissness produces unwanted equations of misconception. At large divisiveness surges from the bowels of laxity onto white sheets of opaque frivolity staining tenants of spiel. Confined within walls of light, ravenous shadows dance between the feet of lacklustre dewdrops shaken from obtuse failures. Liberated toenail speckles, staining woollen stockings of misuse paint dappled maps of neglected incongruity at the back of the guard dogs of humanity. Imprisoned dereliction peers between bars of smoke masking slights-of-hand games of scrabble speaking to war subterfuges behind closed doors. Ousted governors of privateer infusion yearn for the road's dust dissipation opening onto failure gateways of bribery. Fettered by feather dusters of mundane repetitions, abuses of position fling open vaults of kick-back quandaries and honesty becomes mired within the law. Un-caged doves of lucidness twirl on the ends of media cables to mechanizations of deviate-duty subterfuge subliminally. Impeded integrity foams on the decanter poured beer splashes onto misprision actions taken by forceful entry of hatred shattering the safety latch of life.

Morose

Clandestine announcements herald the onset of splenetic petulance. Offset measurements result in scale-tipping concealed fraudulence. Surreptitious billboards subliminally twerk brusque action figures. Equalizations by heavy-handedness grow pessimistic opt-diggers. Covert operations on national media hits exacerbate waspish hearts. Underhanded choleric pronouncements harden charactered pop-tarts. Counterbalanced weights tilt hope into irascible tirades of anger. Balanced morbidity infects the wilful with subversive script danger. Stealthy liars seduce the gratuitous with whispered glum insinuations.

Open doors slam on inquisitive fingers in swift sullen intimidations. Secret societies capitulate testy unions amid off-centred legislators. Overt decisions mask slights-of-hand encapsulating cranky mediators. Undisclosed falsehoods are played close to the chests of gruff tyrants. Blatant unawareness clouds the decisions of always gloomy variants. Furtive proclamations are given only for the ears of the irritably crass. Patent deceit shadows lips leering before morose vanity mirror-glass.

Moonlit Tonic

Copper caldron sits under the full moon's light a hundred facets all aglow.

Its newly hammered surface sparkles in the freshly fallen snow.

Alone, it sits beside no other, waiting, the quiet rustling bear's witness.

Soon calloused hands will deliver a top like no other, mirrored tail of coil, perfect fitness.

Sour mash added, steady fire kindled, the caldron is blackened under the moonlight.

Clear liquid soon thereafter begins to drip falling diamonds of tonic in the snow white.

Caught in a Mason jar's crystal-clear prison waiting its brothers to gather near.

A hundred-quart jars lined up in a row gently set on a rock shelf calloused hands no fear.

Take one down a sample to test Moonlit Tonic must always be the very best.

Master distiller, lawless man's two gentle calloused hands have no time for idle rest.

Swish and spit get past the burn to flavor and vim in a balanced blend.

First batch from a new kettle is not for sale but makes a fine gift for a good friend.

The peak of flavor is matched by none the third batch it is ready for any fling.

Moonlit Tonic has been made just right the very perfect batch is in time for spring.

Runs are now honed to the perfect pitch flavor flows out in a steady drip.

Tonic in spring makes the heart sing songs of love at weddings from each sip.

Mosaic Dance

Azure heavens walk above emerald waters in lullaby whispered joy.

Grape pods glisten with early morning dew green globed eyes so coy. Fields of auburn grass wave welcome to bare feet promenading past. Roads of hard packed ginger pave serpentine adventures that last. Speckling of grey sheds wink invitation to happy feet wondering afar. Carts' wares bounce on skipping wheels into coffee dusted gates ajar. Twinkling eyes crinkle lips of spectators into smiling answers to byes. Sun-kissed noses smell drying posies on assemblages of clear skies. Tesserae of chutney bask in the warm days of Tuscany's summers. Hands, of wrinkly brown, sport brilliant frames of decoupage runners. Freckled bare legs sway to breezes of fun in collages of ballet shouts. Feet of clay break free from timidity and skip within exciting bouts. Days of yore open doors for the imploring of life's holiday rhythmic. Arms undulate in a cadence dance under the Tuscan sun's mosaic.

Mulct

The bard's verb is cheat,

the song weaves deceit

by fraud.

Played with lie forfeit,

at bamboo's wrong beat,

let bawd;

danced, prowled shot defeat.

stab mulct to heart's fleet,

flurry laud.

Stained hard by chicane

acts given guile arcane

penalty.

Arrow's trickery is mundane

awards in fact great pain,

senility.

Duping lads most insane,

bring about writs inane,

infidelity.

Nadir

Strolling through life on our own recognizance, stuck in bottomless
possessions we are drowning in greed blinded by selfishness and ire.

Frolicking with deception on bloody sheets of debauchery, entangled in the
depths of despair we choke oppositions with hate and never tire.

Dancing on the bowed backs of friends we smirk at their servitude as they
fall into an all-time- low, branded as go-getters we smile tyranny.

Cart wheeling across the minds of neighbours we relish their penury as we
hoard golden mists drawn from the nethermost bursts of dupery.

Partaking of rampant under-most illicit drug fantasies, possessed with
desire's addictions we excuse mindless manipulations of the innocent.

Streaming youth into the wealth machine of trafficking we produce our
future at the rock bottom of incurable perverse commencement.

Raising self-consumed zombies that revel in the pits masticating all
correction we turn blind eyes to the sharpening sword of our demise.

Moulding mirror images of our mistaken purposes into unyielding stone
derelicts we grope madly toward the sweet nadir of our surprise.

Nascent

Spontaneous emergence from the primordial goo science tells is true. Like mice from a box of dirty clothes three centuries past lies we rue. Carbon, nitrogen, amino acids, water the cake of life rises on its own. Volcanic stimuli catalyse chemical reactions spring forth seeds sown. Issued from strayed strands of primate DNA man walks by chance. Delusions' words and acceptance speeches rise from happenstance. Denigrations of yore revisit scientists' mistakes of reification indeed. Supposition, fact bending and subversion materialize a chemical seed. Heart beats and foot prints with tails dragging emanate from sea beds. Wisdom deprived scholars spout theory and hypothesis conning fools. Intricate life works mitochondria in the billions are but reified tools. The soup bowl of life has come into being from a stone's evolution. Miscreant guesses create Homo Sapiens' steps in nascent convolution.

Non Sequitur

Awakened at dawn the day to tread my heart is full of joyous dread.
Pandered illicitness scrapped raw my new wound I join soggy bread.
Ungratefulness ran me over in a blue orange bus as I fished for a soul.
Incongruity danced down my spine with icy fingers of fire's hot toll.
Serpentine lassos sprang up from the dust and lifted my lids unhinged.
Leaden raindrops routinely fall down my hollow shoulders, I cringed.

Nonplussed realizations flick barbed tongues of joy into contentions.
Feathered snowflakes hammer my cheeks with searing interventions.
Vacuums full of ethereal thoughts spill happenstance onto life's bibs.
Whispered cadences of vulgarity reveal angry scared accepted quips.

Dust bunny caked artefacts dance in stillness on contemporary glitter. My capillaries gush with exuberant death as hope soaks in me bitter. Streams babble nonsense at the roots of dead oaks that curtsy lies. Desks shout profound slanders in the ear of would-be poetry tries. Similes wrestle periwigs from the knuckles of tech fishermen packets. Broad-moors ooze dandelion florets upon breezes of calming rackets. Mice paws play concertos in rice grain feces surrogated by mirth loss.

Nonsequitur rhymes assault proverbial MFA's with inflexible moss.

Nugatory

Hints dropped on moments of doubt in bombs of harsh vain accusations, songs of delusiveness shot through the hearts of the vulnerable by oboes' subliminal lies, tattoos etched with fire into the exposed flesh of societal manipulations fall into indictments of worthlessness, operettas dance melodies of reduction into the minds of the weak to open gates of uncertainty that whispers of uselessness, cool drinks from the decanter of empty promises squelch the fires of passions for truth, flashcards of covetousness turn content hearts to mad pursuits of fruitless striving that crushes souls, pleasure peddlers gloss over consequences masking their sales pitches of hollowness with glass masterpieces that quickly shatter, timidity becomes stuck to the boot heels of seduction and is dragged into muddled ineffectiveness, life's pages are turned backward by the hands of idle hangers-on and tomorrow gets farther away, media reels of idolatry whir swiftly along in a numbing buzz that invalidates honesty with false indignation at perceived offenses, time's dark void wraps the cloak of acceptance tightly around the throats of the duped until breath passes inconsequentially, lies spoken in repetitious encouragements boast bootless struggles to fertilize abortive ideas within the minds of the gullible, the Father of Lies befriends the unprotected to induce feelings of nugatory to generate slaves to his futility.

Numbed

Awash in subliminal manipulations we are anaesthetized by malice. Elevated bye pride we are insensitive taking our neighbour's chalice. Aflame with self-importance we make unfeeling ruination from love. Foundering through the icy waters of insentience we slaughter a dove. Taking up the fires of inequity with deadened hands we smirk at hope. Locking slavery's iron collar on insensible necks in gloom we grope. Drooling at the altar of Media-ism we are stupefied by empty brains. Beaten by pleasurable influences we board the willingly greedy trains. Sucking down all desires we are frozen to eternal straws of gluttony. Fixed on the ICU bed of comatose indulgence we are stuck in luxury. Seduced by covetousness we are asleep on gold sheets over the poor. Covered by too much information we are numbed to acts that restore.

Nurtured

My knife is rusted,

our hopes are busted,

canted day.

Words badly crusted,

if only we had trusted

light's ray.

Verbs wrongly dusted,

meanings are byte lusted,

open tray.

Your news is packed

in ifs, butts stacked

on dope.

Your finger is whacked,

by bleeds is cracked,

to grope.

Nurture me, ass slacked,

foster me, thought backed

elope.

Nutriment

In love, God gave the ultimate life's bread,

and by the Living Word's steps, He has read

words joyful to all, instructing both great and small

in ways of peaceful paths for feet to tread.

A hand of divine support reaches down

to offer a tug from the sin muck bound

souls' yearning toward a refining spirited learning

of the way to straight-and-narrow's shinning crown.

In hope eyes gaze forever upward longingly

toward the skies' mystery most lovingly,

in search of the face of Christ's redeeming grace

to glue faith robes onto their body very firmly.

A bent knee presents reverence to endless peace,

as contrite hearts bleed, sorrow's bowed heads cease

their flowing tears when grace erases all their fears

and hope blooms eternal at life's ending lease.

Obfuscate

Concealed in flute melodies, subliminal hate spears the unwary through the mind, pooling confusion where joy should abide; shadowed by ill intent the daisies of hope wither in darkness's shade disguised as coats of armor shell shocked deviations from the straight and narrow paths to freedom, feet become mired in umbrage sands that suck faith into the void of deviant behaviors hidden among the roses bordering the sidewalks of indecision, the aroma of crushed petals masks the hidden decay secreted under crisp sheets of social mask wearers bending to the complicated lifestyles of the morally bent opulent praise seeking who cloud truth with their overindulgent mechanizations of the poor and needy that they keep secreted in the closet dust bunnies under their beds of imprisoned empathy that they've removed like last week's dirty underwear of fuliginous speak-easies against their neighbor's shortcomings in order to provide thick mantels of envy to obfuscate their wicked intentions.

Obituary

The final words at the cessation of earthly life give litany to the exploits of the celebrated. The last rights give rise to blossoms of insight. The memorial services tickle the faithless with tendrils of hope. The cenotaphs etched into the stones of timelessness give reminders of firm beliefs. The shrines of memory markers along the interstates of pain shed light upon the forgotten. The mausoleums of the well-preserved give crystal whispered hope of life eternal. The crypts of solidarity are sewn together with the threads of harmonious cherubim concertos. The tombs of the obedient reverberate with echoes of dedicated footfalls. The sepulchers of the saints resound with the testimonies of truth. The vaults of the martyrs cry out with the drops of blood of the faithful. The catacombs, of the forgiven, show the way through the maze of deception and end in the flowing waters of life.

Ocular

Your eyes are jaded,

your vision faded

cloudy whey.

Daggers by night bladed,

piercing the dark pervaded

in grey.

Half lids have shaded,

intense she has waited

for May.

Visual clues have sliced,

though not very spiced

in light.

Optic is groping for Christ,

in corners not sufficed

but bright.

Lamps are mostly diced

without hint to priced

blind sight.

Oeuvre

Sweat bleeds across the brow of the haunted in streaming words of contrition pointing to the handle on the vine draped rusted gates, an arthritic hand gropes blindly for a grasp by which to turn the lock and enter into Opera Omnia's finale, to which scoffers reply in so-many disdainful words that the product failed to inspire indiscretions in the morally decadent to whom they pay homage in slanderous endeavors against the humble composer's triumphal vendetta with the wicked who conspire subterfuges backstage with thug mechanical light engineers' betrayals of queues misplaced along the threads of rhyme weeds tilled from the rows of corn maidens' Demi-pointe shoes during side careers on pestilence bedspreads stained by hated career stepping stones' debaucheries in misplaced trusts for advancement, in order to complete the highest quality output for a flash-bang of applause from ego misogynists holding tryst place cards with which they beat the young at heart lasses, who attempt to contort their life's delusions into a veneer of happiness over a worm eaten core of languished dreams beaten with rods gripped in the hands of bitterness while corpus grandiose matrons force the crippled feet of the needy into pointe-de-feet bawdy trips between the illicit slip-posts of modernists' docked ships sinking into the harbor of timeless innocence rapes, where now the grand culmination of blinded perseverance is your Oeuvre?

Onus

The onus of our crimes committed weighs heavily across our stooped backs
as we trudge blindly along broad easy paths to perdition's ebony gate
glistening in the firelight flickering out of the abyss's maw broken in jagged
condemnations of weaknesses embraced by flaccid arms of hopelessness
because of unrepentant culpability denied with our last breath while
blaming our neighbor's innocence for our guilt to ensure we feel vindicated
of our debaucheries in our own eyes, and try to damn the blameless with
imputations of our liabilities to those who are too meek to protest against
the heinous charges that we lay to their account and shift our ponderous
burdens from our own shoulders striving for relief from blame for murders
of faith against those whom we ill-use for stepping stones to fame and
wealth by which we pave our denunciations of truth and attempt to slip
beneath the consequences of hate while fear swells past recognition our
faults until we beat blindly about ourselves with the heavy hammers of
censure trying to slam those who offer words of encouragement and
empathy, we turn not from our wickedness.

Oppress

Voices of reason are afflicted by angry retorts to pervert the still waters of calm admonitions from those trying to instruct the ignorant in ways of hope that won't fail the feet of the contrite of heart, but the flails from those who choose to tyrannize the meek peel back the layers of empathy to expose the infirmities caused by years of saturation of the mind with repressions of opportunities fought for by the sweaty brows of the truth seekers, how soon now the subjugation veil will be rent apart by the Word of Righteousness who stands for the relief of oppressive misguidance from the honey-tongued father of coercion and breaks the shackle that keeps down the faithful and distills their love through the fires of condemnation burning hotly underneath the cesspools of inhumane dominations masked as freedoms of choice and furtherance of selfish pursuits to the detriment of incongruities of seemingly helplessness.

Ostensibly

The diamond-dust coat glimmers and sparkles with a deceitful shell.

The flashy orange notice is eye-catching and mesmerizes like a bell.

Eyes of innocence cannot penetrate the superficially charged armor.

Seemingly incongruence weaves in and out of hope, a snake-charmer.

Froth with enticing rose petal scales, wickedness hides death's knell.

Royal purple robes veil horrid forms in a delightfully charming spell.

Outwardly appealing, inwardly unfeeling, we mask the shapeless clay.

Softly, ill words evidently bend the truth to the ears that fear to pray.

The façade has been glossed presumably with songs that often fell.

Illusions of apparent acceptance allege obstinately good works to sell.

Shattered mirrors of dreams reflect supposed archaic endeavors' time.

The stilled hearts of loss warp the meanings of lying tongues' rhyme.

Built sandcastles at high-tide reveal meanings of stories' truths to tell.

Lifted veils bare countenances of plots unseen by eyes of hope's well.

Ostensibly awake at the midnight-hour, hearts turn from holding firm.

Minds opened by the Book of Life expose lies that make evil squirm.

Outstretched Arms

Expectation bunnies float across sunbeam checkered flagstones of choice options' grids. Saltwater droplets cascade down quartz smooth cheeks at reprimands harsh word alternate bids. Discovery surprises explode at odd moments startling growing brains into A-ha flashes of joy. Bugger dotted goo-threads stretch down from little red noses attending to personal staged poi. Anticipation fingertips dance over electro-magnetic piano keys, marching out concertos of pain. Weighted pull-ups of forgotten bathroom needs remind that gravity wins a second race to gain. Fervent feet outpace balance and floorboards dance vertical needs that meet horizontal faces. Red welt chins match bruised elbows bent to leverage second attempts at toddler balanced paces. Eager eyes search faraway skies for voices that encourage fourth tries for steps more than two. Soaked bottoms give shock absorption squishes as small buttocks pounce down, faces all blue. Wholehearted thrusts from hands and knees too give proper impetuous for fifth attempt's rise. Streaming rivers splash down as tired legs fail and the tears of trials lament the ever-lost prize. Anticipation's cronies, fear and insecurity cross off hope as little arms stretch up for a boost. Sniveling hiccups render little lips trembling with need in an hour of despair as a lap gives roost. Serenity implodes with rest and security in the arms of known love and peace descends on time. Soft gurgle snores sing lullabies across facades awash with exhaustion's toll for a new rhyme. Tranquility descends over minds set to love's embrace amid learning curves' attempts of reason. Dry butts and full bellies contentment's smile spreads joy across a budding toddler's season.

Overhaul

By the hand of Love we have been fixed,

with greatest care hate has at last been nixed.

Our Master's hand patches us up with fistfuls of sand,

as we bow to grace's open armed love mixed.

By the Tree of Life we are now refitted,

with spirit's rebuilt parts wholly unrequited.

Our desires met with pardonable payments let

hopes' zenith descends to atones all permitted.

By Word of Intercession we are repaired,

with utmost space from guilt, we are spared.

Our shackles shed, our feet freed, given our daily bread,

by faith we take the pierced hand that cared.

By the Mediator's voice we are restored,

overhauled, the Great Mechanic to our ward

remands us to health, revamped our soul's wealth,

by refurbished parts gathered from where they are stored.

Parallax

Bent by the shadows, the face of redemption goes unrecognized by the searching eyes of the unrepentant as they scan the wasteland for hope that eludes their untrained minds and their faith has dwindled to a non-existence in the lost and muddied waters of scientific ignorance rushing around in arrogant delusions of grandeur and pride that dissolve the sands of time from beneath the feet of the wayward who march steadfastly and willingly to death by self-strangulation in a suffocation of indulgence that never ceases and work-o-holics crush all opposition to their golden self-image idolatry faces molded as they plow down their friends and neighbors beneath iron wheels of never slowing train wrecks toward wealth and power in prideful all-acceptance speeches made before bowing grovelers who lick the beads of blood drops from the boot toes of those who choose to cover the truth by hiding their own culpability in matters of murder and puissant mongering by slight-of-hand gestures that distract the vision of those looking indirectly at salvation through kaleidoscopes of displaced trust seen from beneath colorful palettes of misdirection at the deft fingers of the master of parallax.

Parsimonious

Gifts of time and love cost nothing, but the investments reap rewards more precious than gold or jewels in the eyes of the miserly minded.

Children hope for a kind word, a gentle hand of encouragement and a sense of love in their daily isolation; stricken in homes of the blinded.

Bound to scrimpy existences serving their own needs with fervor and generous needle pokes, mothers drool apathy into helpless habits.

Enslaved to frugality of emotions, hidden in a stupor of senselessness by illicit contradictions, fathers recline in the vomit of broken addicts.

Shattered dreams lie at the edges of a son's helplessness on straw beds of despondency stuffed with cheap excuses from parents lost.

Woven tapestries of faith frayed at the edges by the sharp tongues of caretakers smoother a daughter's light source at a very high cost.

Parsimonious acts of selfishness bind the joys of life onto stricken vessels of hopelessness sailing the storm-tossed waves of sons forlorn.

Truth skimping tightens the noose of asinine consequences around the throats of opiate eyed moonwalkers and their children cannot mourn.

Permeated

To grow beyond childishness, we must open our souls to be filled with unconditional Love that surpasses all understanding to bring us peace. To gain wisdom for life we must become infused with the Holy Spirit's instructions that open our eyes to kind acts that never cease. To impart the Gospel to others we must saturate our very beings with the Living Word that opens mouths to utter the Good News with zeal. To offer hope to others we must pervade our every action with loving kindness toward our neighbors despite their faults so they can heal. To plant seeds of conviction we must be diffused throughout with the truth that offers up a beacon of hope into the deepest darkest abyss. To nurture growing faith, we must become interfused with a willingness to listen to instructions and act with unconditional bliss. To give freely of our time and hearts we must first be imbued with patience and empathy toward all who would hide from God's face. To embrace forgiveness to all who wrong us we must be permeated with the refining power of Christ's blood that is the free gift of grace.

Piebald

A coat of many colors for a son with much love was given in hope. Jealousy reared its head, a devastating slide down a slippery slope. Marked by patches of many-colored evil acts, brothers failed to see. Many journeys began with a push into the cistern's depth with a plea. Splatters of guilt spotted a family's binding love, causing a major rift. For the one who loved God seemingly lost to slavery in Egypt to drift. Mottled by good in hopelessness he was trusted to a high place lifted. Growing favor and responsibilities given, he to a favored place gifted. Speckled desires pursued to ill intent, in a wise thought away to flee. Rewarded for right choices by a prison sentence long, he was to be. Turned by grace into a teller of dreams his time fulfilled God's plan. Elevated to the second highest in the land a checkered past to stand. Multi-colored position to dole the gathered corn he dispensed it fairly. Famine widespread many fled to Egypt for bread to live life barely. Piebald and dust covered brothers implored for their food's rations. With a forgiving soul he gave grain with all love's unfailing passions.

Poetaster

In the fall of nineteen ninety-three,

I began a poetaster's trip for free,

but tripped and stumbled, my verses crumbled.

Oh why, oh why do these words fail me?

In the spring of twenty zero, zero and two,

I bumbled words like a worn-out shoe.

With a stubborn pen I began all over again,

to rhyme a few lines before death's due.

A bard-master not yet, but now barely fledged,

my verse has now flown off a maiden edged.

A bardlet tossed on the winds of the lost,

yet I strive to be to my craft pledged.

Preachers and Frogs

Preachers and frogs are pretty much the same they call and call oft times in the rain.

They send out the word to reel someone in, one for lost souls one for a lady friend, many times in vain.

Their voices carry far sometimes loud, sometimes soft, always beseeching imploring their need.

With song they draw forth, eyes fastened, compelling, tire treads crush, pulpits splinter, and they bleed.

Frogs and preachers, they call out in desperation, lights, and wonders untold, fires of passion they fan.

One down the aisle strides Bible thumping, the other in the moss jumping, hoping to avoid the frying pan.

Preachers and frogs call out unto the night, imploring, seeking they try to draw in the lost and seeking.

Green skins glisten, bushy brows drip with sweat, ladies fanning, little faces over pews peeking.

Voices lifted in song the tent flaps reverberate the sounds outward the croaks bellow in query.

Fire and brimstone is to bring the souls in, or thrums through the water are to call in a lady friend leery.

Little eyes widen, hell's gate painted on the tent's walls, strong legs proceed as croaks courtship is given.

Courtship draws to an end suitors' sounds echo, preaching reaches a pinnacle crescendo the night riven

Little hands loosen round the frog's belly, preacher a deep breath taken pauses for effect.

Big green frog leaps free, down the aisle hops franticly, spies round bellied preacher and croaks abject.

Presage

A word bodes most ill,

it signifies a chill,

to pay.

As song augurs spill,

it gives mostly a quill,

a dray.

Pulled by verse until,

a portend is real,

not splay.

A betoken is given,

to teach all are driven,

in two.

Prophesy has striven,

with many the forgiven,

not few.

To foretell is livin',

presage may be unforgiven,

to rue.

Putrid

The wealth of Midas is nothing more than decayed morality that is taken into the heart of wrecked intentions crumpled onto heaps of the decomposed grandeur fallen from the shoulders of the incongruent diamonds corrupted by being dipped into rotten souls' endeavors' from ill-gotten gains from rancid investments in hatred of neighbors' good deeds which they disparage as wasting money, time and effort that could be better served by throwing them into vile underhanded acts of theft, fraud, and murders, at the hands of the abased who stir the vats of life's hopes mixing in noxious ill acts that befoul the good intentions of the deceived with vindictive gain oriented hammer blows that shatter the glass beakers holding fetid samples of immoralities dabbled in by the seeming pillars of the community who lie to themselves every day and their ruinous examples lead the simple minded down roads of finality ending in the putrid bath houses steaming with the ruined lives of the wealthy dead.

Quaff

The uninspired guzzle life's swill with gusto as they dabble in inconceivable
ignorance's broken promises fractured by self-crime.

The deluded toss down hopeless acts of ego feathering to build warring
images of power from posers that give waste even-time.

The proud drain mugs of sarcasms spouted into the voids of earwax
peddlers who build towers of uselessness by catching the ears of loss.

The powerful swig multi-colored teas of insipidness mixed with bitterness
from years of isolations at the top of nothing as main boss.

The lonely gulp flaming sweat shots from the driven subservient cattle
lowing in dark pastures of slavery to work blinded by oft pains.

The crowing heralds of death gulp their last sweet lungs of air free from
doubt but crushed by guilt not admitted to as sky's tear rains.

The broken at last see clearly as they clinch tight their lips against truths
uttered into the void of their own minds that are locked tight.

The bitter revelations will have to be quaffed by the throats of the
condemned that refuse to repent of their wickedness and take flight.

Quasi

A painted-on smile and a fake empathetic demeanor mask the true heart of those who profess to be Christian heralds of the Good News. A seemingly benevolent agenda hides the horrendous acts of attrition that undermine the hard-working truth gardeners who hold firm views. An apparently benign teacher weaves words of corruption into the fabric of a sermon to corrupt the ignorant with false prophetic words. An outwardly angelic countenance glows with the darkness of heavily masked hatred intentions bound into caked-on makeup of goat herds. A superficially charged zealot astounds the masses with acclamation shouts to misdirect the ears of wayward minded sheep who in-mingle. An assimilated child takes on the blood spotted garments of his adopted role-models who slash the innocent by sharp tongues' tingle. An evidently wavering effort to chide the lost falls short of the goal of admonishment of the guilty to non-offend the self-righteous. A Quasi-Christian need not apply for consideration of forgiveness because of an insincere admission of guilt only on the surface as bias.

Quench

To crush is bladed,

poetic lives jaded

by fate.

An end is oft faded,

into blurry pervaded

words' hate.

Can't terminate waded

in bloodbath are mated

but late.

To ruin is by chosen

act subdued in frozen

rhyme deaths.

Sated palates are woven

allayed Ambrosian

relief breaths.

To quench fire's cloven

tendril's finger ill coven

hollow meth's.

Queue

Broken on stones of a far-flung shore, rows of faith wait in the way. Slain in the teeth of gluttony, file and rank simpletons give easy sway. Fallen into the hands of deceit, the lines of expectancy are bent anew. Gathered at the fields of slaughter, the un-championed are oft askew. Swept into a lineup of despairing misguidance, the lost weep old days. Packed into waiting their turn, for wealth the greedy join devil plays. Refrains of hate form lines of ill-sonnets that rouse the fires of need. Herded together, caused to get in lines of jostling goats tears bleed. Dominoes placed patterns of decay line up ready for the finger's fall. Stacked in the queue records of deeds done are to be played one'n all.

Quisling

Breakaway pride runs rampant over the meek daisies and they wither. The recreants conceit brushes aside timid dandelions who float hither. Mutineers force the compassionate to walk the plank and they drown. The renegades scalp the kindhearted and their life's blood runs brown. Seditionists plot hatred against the torch bearers who fall to the dark. The apostates conspire with abhorrence against the benevolent in lark. Defectors turn aside the good intentions of the empathetic unto death. The turncoats amass ill-gotten gains to smoother the generous' breath. Deserters flee retribution from the armies of truth marchers' who die. The rats swarm the stores of the prudent to ravage the bread for a lie. Traitors practice intrigue in the dark to hide their culpability by night. The quisling seeks destruction of the worthy working for what is right.

Quittance

Reparation cannot be made by good deeds performed without love. Heavy debt cannot be discharged by random acts of void selflessness.

Amends do not count if the heart is filled with retribution thoughts. Compensation is inadequate when begrudgingly given with a grimace. Redress falls short when perceived wrongs are harbored in ill hearts. Indemnification with jealousy fails of its release and pride prevails. Remuneration in the flesh counts as nothing on the scales of justice. Expiation with a begrudging attitude crushes the hand of the greedy. There is but One that gives adequate payment at the final settlement. His atonement pays all debts for those willing to admit his grace offer. The just recompense for our guilt was taken out on His innocence. Proper restitution which we could not pay dripped red from His hands. Reprisal for our transgressions may now be circumvented if we ask. Quittance is ours if we but stretch out our spirit to accept the free gift.

Quod

Immured in the bosom of fallen leaves, peace exceeds time's attrition.
Interned in a chlorophyll of spring bars, rebirth tops hope's rendition.
Circumscribed by the vines of summers' wild, revival sings full joy.
Incarcerated by a stone wall of winter's snow, rest does not annoy.
Imprisoned within the grip of faith, freedom blooms a carpet of bliss.
Confined in the arms of leniency, a melody caresses lips in a soft kiss.
Constrained by conscious' empathy, wrongs are forgotten in the mist. Jailed in the dungeons of cumulus cloud tops, the angels open a list. Quod inside the pearly gates of eternity, Love's tears fall at the end. Bastille waits at the lower gate, after a broad and easy path to lend.

Raconteur

Words in blue drift on breezes of yesterday as mists across the moor. Limericks in red blaze through tomorrow like a wildfire in grassland. Folklore in green sprout in the forests of dreams as seeds in rich loam. Oral histories in bronze reflect the lights of deeds like heroes of old. Chanted instructions in orange rage in young hearts as zeal to action. Tales in brown puff into the air of indifference like dust from the trail.

Orations in azure flash above still waters as northern lights over snow. Narrations in gold gleam through the night like tokens of hope flakes. Conversations in royal purple spill over dignitaries as bent wig-locks. Raconteurs' canvases are ready to be painted by the master's pen.

Replete

Come to the table of grace and forgiveness that abounds with Love. Accept the plate of redemption and be completed with inclusion. Grasp the backpack of salvation and be well supplied for the future. Take hold of the hand of the Slain and gain abounding peace. Embrace the truth of the gospel and enjoy a teeming, fantastic life. Partake of the banquet of the Living Word and be full of expectation. Plant yourself in rich soil of giving and yield an overflowing harvest. Take up your cross of obedience and be rife in spreading the Love. Submit to the will of Faithfulness and be sated in with divine manna. Hold firm until the end and become replete with all that matters.

Riant

Sunshine and daisies make young lambs frolic like jovial crazies. Meadowlarks' songs trill through the mists slicing a jolly thrill. Shadows and trillium offer maroon smiles a boon to William. Carolina Wrens' twitters and tweets bring ears unbound gleeful treats. Mists over the creek dance where sunbeam's jocund clasps meet. Catbirds' mews knit gay tricks into mittens of off-the-map fondue wit. Thunderstorms penetrate covered ears letting blithe words free fears. Jay's squawks jar pensive minds into festive avalanches of time rocks. Spinning breezes dance in yesterday's leaves to mirthful happenstance. Titmice rally in tandem rhythms over the lighthearted feed fandom. Fantastic visions bleed merry tears across artificial landscapes freed. Riant hearts await the key of timeless Cross tumblers' new life spree.

Roué

Broken, slumber's blissful repose eludes the waves of a guilty consciousness's pursuits of infidelity dollars gained becoming a millionaire's dream of an elusive billion dollar-club inclusion by debauched man's gleaming eyes as he hungrily devours life's precious-moments and children wail through atrocious acts of violence against the innocence of hope's lost enticements and scattered thoughts rain down in droplets of suppressed empathy from the shredded humanity of a dissipated man's coin chasing by means of a top-dog career careening into censored loneliness denied at every opulent party where schmoozing and groveling become second nature that a pinnacle of life may someday be achieved before the rot of death ends the self-indulgent lives of those seeking an empty heart and an overly full investment account achieved through the death destruction by financial ruin of all that oppose the survival of the fittest as a degenerate mind plays roulette with any who have crossed paths and may be picked clean of any surviving flesh gold to swell the coffers of greed through a dissolute man's mind games of never ending business transactions, as the day of my next wealth jackpot stares at me though the somewhat mist mirror while I shave and preen as any red-blooded American Roué must do at the start of a new day.

Rouse

The eon's leviathan slumbers fitfully in the void between the stars.

The holes in his fabric of peace twinkle until he moves in dreams. Ruptured light pours into the vastness of nothing as death stalks Mars. The noise of inequity grows louder till incessant roaring life screams. Provoked by the unrestrained technical leaps a death emissary moves. He sheds stars as tears from a bereft child's cheeks, the cosmos splits. Awakened from an epoch of dormancy destruction by hate proves. Light fails at the outer corners of the universe as the Milkyway shifts. Revived by the long groaning malevolence from Terra, a fissure runs. Implosions suck all matter into the nothingness of many black holes. Quickened through the age-old return to wickedness is etched in puns. To rouse our own demise is our chosen folly and we crush our souls.

Rove

Misguided feet drift from the path of truth into oblivious ignorance. Wayward hands grasp tails of arrogant roamers into worthless esteem. Errant eyes stare into golden idols of rambling worshipers of idiom. Ill-advised minds seek after maundering illusions of opulent lifestyles. Unruly hearts beat to cadences of lusty circumambulations in shadow. Rash legs run to the offers from those who traipse after empty deeds. Reckless arms gather indulgence from free ranging envoys of death. Foolish ears listen to the misogynistic lies from the lips of wanderers. Lost souls rove in the darkness of the abyss seeking illusive answers.

Rustic

To walk in truth is to walk oft alone through the garden of grace. Country life grows one's spirit as a seedling in rich soil of God's race. To toil a good venture the air must be full of iniquitous free cleanness. Bucolic wayfarers play fiddles of empathy to see a sword's keenness.

To sweat for a just cause entails a firm resolve to keep a right path. Pastoral farmers tend fields of justice to stave off the righteous wrath. To strive for excellent habits requires a heart strung to faithful ways. Provincial builders wield pegs of love to carry past a child's phase. To attempt a virtuous road, one must rely solely on the Spirit's hand. Rural durability is gained by perseverance's trial learned to withstand. To offer a disciples' conviction a choice of selflessness is a must. Rustic living opens opportunities that bind conclusions for the just.

Sacrosanct

There is but one doorway to the most holy presence of God. Without acceptance of the gift of grace the door remains locked on the outside. The only key is recognition and faith in Christ. To stand at the door and listen for his knock requires an ear to listen to truth. Before the key will turn in the lock a contrite heart must confess the many willful acts of inequity that the flesh has undertaken. With receiving Christ's gift, turning from sin and pleading guilty to all charges the revered feet of God become approachable. Once in the sacred inner chamber of Love no sin can penetrate the stone walls of protective inclusions. As an adopted child of God, a soul has wrapped itself in the armor of forgiveness and becomes untouchable by Satan's filthy hand. The shower of Christ's blood is the only solvent powerful enough to cleans the soul to the proper whiteness to become sacrosanct only through the acceptance of God's gift without which no amount of good works can even dim the blackness of our endeavors.

Sage

The hope frontier whispers enticements into the ears of the Truth seekers who hold answers to the imprisonment of societal malfeasance. Across the great smoke enshrouded mountains of tomorrow lie lands of mystery and unknown opportunities behind the iron gates that may be opened by risky choices. The sagacious decedents of Knowledge explorers hold to a zeal for the far horizon that is opened by a slight push from the controlling hands of oppressors crowding through the trees of newly built cabins of escape with their ever-broadening governmental subversions to entrap the dictatorially ignorant. Onward feet are driven to seek abstruse answers to life's ever widening mysteries that the suppressors work diligently to squelch with never ceasing stockades of laws designed to enslave the masses. Clever independence weavers thread cloaks of striking color oddities to confound the eyes of tyranny with the well-manicured fabric of societies' ignorant milling about the fringe. While the sheepdogs of faithfulness are working to herd the cats of futility who continually try to release a tide of profound offensiveness onto the other misled, who would murder their own freedom for the gold of Midas, progress is stalled. Perceptive truth seekers, all the while, place levees of caution before the onrushing flood of hoodwinked idealists being pumped out of the repetitively conning facilities of higher education onto the condemned rails of treacherous sophistry deluding the unknowingly bereaved. Timid latecomers move with caution into their lukewarm wisdom and sway on the edge of a razorblade at the margin of hope between truth and fabrication balancing both worlds on their scales of hesitancy. But the acumen saturated, who have learned active fortitude, plunge forward into the tangled jungle of unknown circumstance attempting to stay ahead of the unwise who congregate within forts of shared manic beliefs to hide their confusion behind mass hysteria. The slightly knowledgeable, but unaware, are pushed in all directions by the lapping high tide of foreign ideologies swamping their genuineness and are piled onto refuse heaps of happenstance like lost grains of sand washed beyond time and place among the innumerable betrayed. Pedantic monarch worshippers herd the marginally fractured into penned cities' of easily manipulated crowd mentalities to control the weak-willed followers of delusion. Esoteric memories invade the dreams of the despoiled by history repeating accords signed again for the four thousandth time barring collective thinkers from free associations that may release their captivity from the iron silk of social spider webs at the mercy of domination minded politicians. Pen strokes behind closed doors, amid the darkened halls, of deal deliberators bind the recondite together within their framework of conspiracy and remain in control of the weak-willed fodder for their high gain investments in human bondage machines. The exploring feet, of the erudite elite forces, plunge future-ward attempting to stay ahead of the ever-expanding ignorance that suffocates all independent wills with the cloying smoke from bottles of confused and muddled minds that ever seek new memberships. The sage of any age must stay ahead of the hope and faith murderers who stalk the fringe dwellers to fulfill lusts for more herd animals to message egos already bursting with arrogant new found wealth until drowning in the Oceans of socialistic wellbeing-wishers who at the very last offer nothing to assuage the swelling tide of apathy that leads to a new frontier of nothing more than foul despite.

Sassafras and Teaberry

Thirst is a tromp through the woods without a drop of water

Heat swelters down humid air tightening its grip as the kiln of a potter.

Up a dry holler and over the ridge I go not even a bead or drop on the moss.

Hog back ridge is bone dry as well nothing to slack my thirst remove this cross.

At every ancient spring I stop probe with questing fingers but no dampness I find.

I look up, the skies are clear not hint of thunderstorm the heavens are not kind.

My trek stretches before my eyes the end not yet even in sight.

The day's frolic has become an unending search; sun's rays weigh down its hot might.

I trudge along lips stuck like bald tires in the thick mud.

My tongue is now useless no moisture does it impart if there'd only been a flood.

Water would have been pooled to find every holler would have offer.

But alas no rain since July the parched ground groans for water from heaven's coffer.

Another mile behind me and finally a small respite I find, benefactor, but no drink.

A slender sassafras tree stands in my path quick snap young shoot lips open from a brink.

The sweet tangy sap brings blessed saliva to a broil at least lips can be wetted.

With sharp cracks two more young limbs in my pocket, I have netted.

Another ridge behind and a holler before, but no water I have found.

At least the north face is cooler a small gift of the mountain, where am I bound?

Oh, yea to Aunt Rebecca's for a fresh pie slice.

Just a few steps farther a boon again mountain teaberry leaves shine, how nice.

Shriek

Flung, torn, shredded from the paths of truth ripped and frayed as the edges of a paper ripped from the spiral bound notebook of life. Wander lost among the confusion of lies and deceit. Challenged deferred to the end-of-life responsibility has been murdered. A slow painful death at the hands of irresponsible pleasure seekers slaughtered by ever-growing lusts truth has become ineffectual. Noah's bane reborn resurrected by the history challenged ignorant of past mistakes blissfully happy follows the light of the fallen one into darkness. Damned by an ever-spiraling weight of blame we place on the innocent to avoid self-incrimination. Objects are responsible people are not. Circumstance causes evil perpetrated by the puppet controlling the puppeteer. We dance on the stings of incompetent lies of self-control. Abandoned, the innocent are given over to those who would consume all that is good. Eaten by the ravenous wild hogs' responsibility has been defecated out into the muck of our fantasized enlightenment. Fallen, leapt, and plunged willingly into the abyss of the joyous raptures of Hell. The hand of life is extended to all who stand at the very brink. Hate trodden, spit upon and ridiculed to death and beyond by the lies of the ignorant learned. History repeated in an ever-downward spiraling pattern. Wandering and alone by choice we slap the outstretched hand that holds eternal joys. Evaluate before the plunge take hold and clasp tight the truth. Recognize the King's crown of thorns, open the doorway to life and take firm hold of Love's outstretched hand and be snatched from the abyss of perpetual hate. Become snatched from the maw of eternal death and shriek with glorious joy instead of true terror's first cry.

Snowflakes and Soot

The soft gentleness of the falling flakes quietly rustles.

The day's duty calls slumbers depart breakfast preparations bustles.

The cook stove is cold the fire's embers slumber in the ashes.

The aged hands work in a few pieces of bark and kindlin from lard pail stashes.

A gentle breath coaxes the lone ember softly the glows deepen.

A tendril of smoke a bunny of soot rises up the flue it goes creepin.

Patience of Job no match to waste the cracked lips persist.

A flicker a spark small blue gold flame withering tongues insist.

A blazing fire is laid the oven glows hotter snowflakes glitter on the window pane.

Hands move with eighty years' practice no thought given no waste or strain.

Chicken breaded, apples sliced, biscuit dough kneaded.

Eggs lay ready, cast-iron pan seated, lard on the stove heated.

The day's light not yet broken the eastern skies.

Snow is now layered on the window like ice cream on pies.

Potatoes now pealed waiting their turn, chicken browning in hot oil spattering.

Chill is now driven out into the morn, teeth still now longer chattering.

Oven ready biscuits formed; tops brushed with yesterday's bacon renderings.

Rising, browning, cracking, aroma is wafting floor to ceiling in its meanderings.

Smells abound mouthwatering scents overflowing permeating every room.

Little beds rattling little feet pattering on the plank floors scurrying for warmth soon.

Kitchen is now toasty the dining room too night shirts are trailing.

Little faces smiling from their eyes sleep departed little noses smelling.

Stubby fingers are reaching for samples, tastes, morsels snatched secretly.

Old eyes sparkle pretending not to have seen the gay pilfering allowed discreetly.

Soot and ash on the snows from the breakfast fires mingle.

The children stand laughing cold toes warming fingers alive now with a tingle.

Sparrows

The chirp, chirp, chirp in the soft morning light heralds the new day's dawn. Numbered, known counted to the very least celebrated life's marvelous songs. The moss gives testimony of the night's passing. Bright green fronds sing the darkness's ending. Seeds and beetles feed the tiny mouths. All are counted, numbered, and known. The tree's leaves in the early light whisper truth heard in the sparrow's song. The hawk's cry, the dove's coo, in harmony with the whispered truth's acknowledgment of life, give proof to the abundance of love. Counted, treasured gifts to the poor, all are more valuable than golden hoards. Butterflies on the buttercups glowing in the sunlight are sparkling witnesses of the final hours. All numbered from the egg are named in intimate contentment of the times. The final hour counted in milliseconds of sand grains falling one at a time through the hourglass of the eons. The final day's dawn the brightest in ten thousand years gives the final light to the unknown dying. Celebrate the rebirth of death unto new life forsaking the lie given at the garden. Fruit and sparrows, trees and flowers, tall grass, and sweet herbs essence waft truth among the stars. All numbers are known, counted as the stars, named fêted with the stripes of love. Birthed by love eons past through the gates of forsaken delivery abandoned reason. At each sparrow's fall and at each star's naming the song of life is sung through time and space until the eon's ending.

Spider Web Cries

Come into my pleasures and hang here with me. Freedom waits for your first grasping hand. Step into my parlor and feel the sweet dreams. They are free for the taking just come and see. Pleasures untold you will find on my threads. Light here so softly and be bound in my bed. Joyous release I offer to thee. So, reach out one finger and place it here beside me. On the hammock free of cares, I will rock you to a pleasant lullaby. Come into my parlor and see for yourself, freedom waits there for you, you will see. Sweet words of praise and flattery go far. Enticement and temptation lead steps along a broad thread. Easy to step onto, hard to step from beguiled by the easy swallowed lies. Charmed with a song of the most beautiful kind, alluring, inviting it leaves none behind. Falsehoods abound with what we want to hear. We hearken and hasten ignoring all fears. In truth we know they are lies but do not care. Search for all our desires leads to entrapment. Hung by our feet in the webs of deceit, wrapped in threads we have woven too tight no escape can we find from the night. We are now stricken with venom of the senseless kind lulled into slumber thinking it sublime. Fears are all sated and forgotten in dreams. Blissfully happy we hang caught in the darkest night. Right up to the stab of the deathly spike we dream our silly pleasures believing all lies. Liquefied in the end our life sucked slowly out, Spider Web Cries release no sound in death's silent night.

Spring Time on Laurel Fork

The does stand guard with ever watchful eyes.

The fawns run kicking and jumping no danger do they spy.

Hawks shrill cry, cardinal's quiet plucking last year's berries everything anew.

Frost on the grass sparkling with sun's fire, a restful sound is the dove's morning coo.

Hesitant chirp chirp of a half-thawed cricket.

The morning mists swirl between the trees and among the thicket.

The creek babbles softly along descending every more quickly.

The minnows dart ever watchful for a meal under the ice crystals so prickly.

The stillness broken by the jackhammer of a woodpecker's incessant pounding.

The thrum causes my heart to try to keep pace in my ears ever sounding.

A powder blue sky swirls by above me the sun to my right the moon to my left.

High cirrus clouds waft by like the mists among the thorns they are rift.

The cows are bawling ready to be milked.

The pail rattles loudly hoping the milk not to be spilt.

First walk through the frost dotted grass then the dew in the sunlight.

I trudge steadily on shoes soggy wet to my knees.

Thoughts of honey and hot fresh biscuits bring my mouth to a smile.

Fresh cow pies by the gate, mud past my ankles the last steps like a mile.

The day's milk to bring home is a chore I am told.

But with fresh butter on my biscuit and honey and with milk I wash down, a great day to unfold.

To milk the cows is no chore especially in spring.

The bounty is plentiful the reward refreshing that a little work I bring.

A smile and a laugh are the greatest treasure.

Sunlight and springtime on Laurel Fork bring the most pleasure.

Starlight

The first twinkle at dusk is herald of diamonds strewn through a fiery
universe divine.

As the mists rise, the breath of earth exhaled on a cold winter's night a veil
to beauty unbound.

The glittering grows as the ebony backdrop of the sky's stage falls fifteen
billion years of prime?

Fiery white, sterling silver tinkling soundlessly above, eyes look up
dreamily ransomed expound.

Dark light slumbers behind the twinkles waiting hunger gnawing the wind
biding the proper time.

Mutely death stalks the shadows appointed to reap a gruesome harvest
silent leaf falls no sound.

He who is last comes first the frost given gift reflected diamonds in the grass
withered rhyme.

Time without record of things forgotten is lost, unfolded bidden come forth
to life's flaming mound.

Gifts of hope journeys hinted offered not accepted but free none the less
unshackled from crime.

Lights burn away the inky blackness of hate as cloth held to the flame holes
of a bloody crowned.

Starlight the gift of the night skies far beyond earthly treasures what do we
value in our prime?

Blazing hosts bear witness to truth unchanging once dipped in the blood we are cleaned, found.

Diamonds more worth than gold we need just stretch out a hand to grasp a love most sublime.

Flashing light from above reflected below sparkling colors all aglow beckon us out of the ground.

Reborn dust to dust returned drawn up again from the deep, the tomb bathed the scent of thyme.

Choices to make starlight to consider accept wisely or deny foolishly the offer this time round?

Steer Fork Jig

The twang of a banjo and the hum of an old guitar blended harmonies sound

Thump of boot and swish of dress twirl and stomp feet move on the old barn floor round n round.

Arms entwine and smiles boast of happy times and joy lets loose.

The caller's sharp bark instructions given bodies dip and twirl tighten up the noose.

Knees rise high, hats are doffed arms' length held, heads bowed with a hand to hip.

Ladies curtsey dress tails lifted from the dust held tightly little fist steady the quick dip.

Music tightens quickens with each beat the caller barks more urgently now the command.

The clap boards reverberate while music embraces the challenge goes out from Steer Fork Band.

The pulse quickens and feet hasten the pace picks up and movements flow.

Sweat drips from noses flaring breath comes ragged now wait the end feet to reap and mow.

The crop of the dance culminates builds to the harvest joyous songs plant the first step garner the last.

The music ceases stings are silent feet stop faces glowing hands clapping for that which is just past.

The Steer Fork Jig has rung its last feet stroll to stools and tables at hand dad leads mother.

Ladies go one-way gents the other sweat is wiped from the brows of one dabbed from the other.

Talk begins in a low murmur smiles still plaster every face turned up breaths to catch a moment to wait.

The band meanders, turning milling about a few hands carry flasks to lips a small nip thirsts to abate.

A quick break, breaths caught sweat barely dried the music begins again the first step seeded.

The caller rises, feet move forward of their own responding melodies explain the movements needed.

Expressions life force shown explained in the movement and words hard works culminate.

The months of labors are mostly passed by and the time of bounty has fallen time to celebrate, ruminate.

Stricken

The depths of our narcissism nail us to the walls of slavery.

Blinded by our own deceit we ignore advice from our closest friends' bravery.

Stricken without acknowledgement, blinded, our eyes no longer see.

Sought but not found we look in the wrong places ignoring God's plea.

Lost we refuse to be found, armed with denial, we defend against Love.

Wrapped in darkness, plunged into the abyss we refuse what is from above.

Impaled with ignorance the more knowledge we gain, utterly stricken.

The soup of our desires we boil through life our own quagmire we thicken.

Hate masked in tolerance but no forgiveness offered we damn those different.

Woven intricately into the fabric of our despair till enemies we become equivalent.

From freedom to slavery the broad path leads us in a fevered race.

Narcissism binds us into faithless chains forward we rush into its cold embrace.

Slain is love for any other as we fall quietly into the maw of midnight.

From the light we flee in a hurried rush as terror snatches us into a heinous flight.

To turn toward truth and the narrow path is the last choice before our final fall

We best make the choice soon and walk truth's road, God's answer to evil's call.

Sunshine and Blackstrap

The early fall sunbeams hold warmth enough to thaw the core.

The cane gathered the mule ready the mill cleaned ready for the pour.

The fire is hot the kettle is shined waiting the sap to render.

All hands gather round the ole' cane mill belly up to the tarnished fender.

Ole' Blue now tethered to the turnstile he knows his pace.

Each task allotted all here know tis an all-day race.

The first stalks in Ole' Blue moves forward without a word spoken.

The light mist wafts by as the sunlight glistens heat as if for the day's token.

The sun creeps up as Ole' Blue plods round.

The green juice starts as a drip then a trickle soon a half bucket maybe a pound.

The first sled full is emptied the second waits near ready to be fed.

Each knows his task carry, feed, pull, stir, skim long time before bed.

The day's task has just begun Ole' Blue twitches an ear at the crew.

Laughter at jokes fills the air, songs lifted up nothing here to rue.

Dinner time comes but no break is given no shade she finds.

Fried chicken leg in left hand work with the right no one minds.

Afternoon drags shoulders grow weary, arms ache, backs stoop.

Foam beings to roll in earnest now the skimmers make a troop.

The day's work nears its end the final lap is in sight.

Ole' Blue senses his task most complete his last laps become a flight.

Granny comes teetering flour sack lined wheel barrow full of jars.

Gray head bobbing, jars a clanking, her old hands are strong but show many scars.

Table cloth spread crisp with starch just to her liking.

Jars spread five rows deep the whole length; to fill them all takes much hiking.

Blackstrap jar filling is her chore.

You best not get in the way or your knuckles will be sore.

Taken

Taken before their time, so we believe them to be, lost for a season to those who mourn. Taken by the hand to the place of rest we cannot fathom the reason. Taken away in the prime of perceived life our hearts are left tattered. Taken from life as babes we weep in ignorance. Taken out of our arms to be cradled in pure love waiting we lament our loss. Taken out of time and place lost to our eyes unseeing we grieve without knowing. Taken from our clutches as we try to hold tight, we weep for ourselves as we grasp for understanding. Taken are our candles of hope and we wander in darkness. Taken and torn in heart and mind we hold vigilance against the hopeless despair of the evil one. Taken with anger we rage against life's seeming unfairness. Taken with grieving over our own uselessness we struggle to breathe. Taken by anguish our heads slip quietly into the murky depths of despondency. Taken away half our soul was ripped asunder and left to be trampled underfoot by the yapping hyenas of deceit. Taken by the hand of God for a purpose of good we cannot see we question why. Taken our cries are hurled out and swallowed in the darkness between the stars. Taken our hearts ache with loss unimaginable. Taken in despair we may drown in whispers of the evil one. Taken back if we hold tight to the light of faith we are comforted. Taken into the shelter of love if we hold tight to our hope, we are relieved. Taken home to be reunited once again if we accept the offer of love we are redeemed.

Thanksgiving

Breath, blood, and heart life's forces like the flares from sol.

All gifts are from above without which we are nothing, dust.

Cell's designs of Love's life flow stamped made as if a doll.

Give thanks this day for life's a gift freely given, just.

Breathe for joy wrapped in happiness not our own found.

Sunlight and starlight shine upon all formed, conformed to His will.

Be thankful for all; remember from where we come a small dust mound.

Nothing more than a breath of life on the chafe from the Miller's mill.

Rain and sun on the day's crops growing new life is given freely.

Abundance is overflowing with milk and honey rich beyond measure.

In our mirror's image we praise, thank, and worship our own labor weekly.

Why do we believe ourselves to be the source of all our treasure?

Too quickly we forget our own breaths are counted, numbers of health.

Allotted according to His plan, they are gifted openly to all.

Our thanks we withhold hoard as a miser his wealth.

To thank our true Benefactor divine seems beyond our grasp, we fall.

Fail, crumple, ruin, heart ache and disease for all we ask why.

If hearts remain closed, eyes unseeing we face the doom of our construction.

Our eyes we must turn heavenward thanksgiving better be loosed, let go glad cry.

Give heartfelt thanksgiving every day to God above or face alone our destruction.

The Fields of Yore

The day's dust to tread,

work and sweat each morning with dread.

Up two hours before dawn,

grub the fields till the last light is gone.

Lunch from a lard pail,

hard tack and beans without fail.

Rows of corn without end,

crops untold too many to tend.

From dark to dark the day is done,

labor without end, where is the fun?

The days pass each as before,

chore after chore till my back is sore.

Days to years, years tenfold,

life most gone a story untold.

Time at last to shed some light,

to any that listen I tell my plight.

The young could learn a better path,

if only they would attend without wrath.

Work should be a glad affair,

a pleasure a laugh for all to share.

The Lost

Abandonment of reason is a response to fear, disjointed, random, and lost.

Those who desire power foster fear, terror, hate, and do not count or care the cost.

The People relinquish power when fears are fed with lies, they are subjugated, enslaved, lost.

The powerful revel in their iniquity, wallow in self-proclaimed piousness, freedoms are tossed.

Democracy has been taken, stripped by fear and avarice, usurped by the powerful, lost.

The masses in ignorance led blindly to deaths by lies, fools of power insatiable lies glossed.

A free state is only free so long as the people rule, so lies are given to seduce the lost.

Hunger for power, control by the governing authorities, taken by lies, illusions, diamonds of frost.

Cold encased, bound in iron shackles, hands willingly extended locking their own shackles, lost.

Big government binds the willing slaves to fear, controls, grows fat in power, it cannot be crossed.

Money spent we do not have a chain around the albatross's neck weighted unto death, lost.

Tyranny runs rampant given over freely by the fearful governed by lies, societies exhaust.

The charge to government is to be austere, penny-wise rigorous principles, strictures not lost.

Peoples at time must shake loose seek enlightenment and truth take task the powerful to accost.

The wolves are in the sheep pen, ravenous thrashing about slashing those in ignorance lost.

Do the sheep smell the slaughter of truth, or do they listen to the media's lies blood embossed?

The oppressors exult in the gore of the fall, engorged for a time until in their own vomit lost.

The powerful have seduced and bound us all by their bloody revelry, freedom is sauced.

Truth's Freedom

Freedom is elusive at best temporal within reach but never caught.

Truth abounds for all to see, elusive for many their sight clouded by what they have been taught.

Aristotle, Pasteur, Edison, and Columbus what if they had held to the science of their day?

What truth to now have, a flat earth, a leech for a doctor, candle for light, stars circle earth, say?

If we all follow science teachings without question, what would we now have, what truth's price?

Truth stands to believe or deny, unchanged from the start unquestioned once, twice, thrice.

Freedom is here in truth to be found who has wisdom let him hear, who has love let her see.

Truth is near hidden our hands cover our ears, sight blinded by tears, no truth where will we be?

Truth's freedom is free for the taking it requires recognition and a willing embrace.

Where now those who can see lost in the herd, sheep mentality we flounder lose truth's race?

Freedom's true meaning is not easily discerned a clear eye, open heart, wise mind are required.

Where now those who seek, study, question the status quo, in the hustle and bustle mired?

Too busy to care, too much work to see, truth escapes all who, through life's struggles, flees.

Freedom is our God given right the Constitution speaks of it outright but we have lost it in the trees.

Blindly we see that before our feet, in front of our noses, in our hands, but not any truth.

Lost in freedom to struggle and work, riches and wealth hoard we never read Job or Ruth.

The truth must be sought studied and pursued daily or else we are seduced by the lie.

Freedom is only in truth and love, not in the lies and promise of riches, now is the time to cry.

Tyrant

Smiling face twinkling eye mask of death unrecognized hidden bought by terror dreams of fire.

Lies easily swallowed by eager hearts, lies are sweet when words utter our desire.

Appeals are for the poor, riches to spread, wealth abound for all a gift offered without price.

Hungry eyes seeking every groping for something without effort or cost death's toll twice.

Rome renewed pursued, money paid bought with honey and promise an immortal contract made.

Shadowy death stalks the gates of victory, waiting, much is owed; debt of first dirt is in the spade.

The grave comes slow unrecognized an abyss of blackest depth hollowed by our own votes.

Lewd money, soft words seduce we follow to our slaughter blindly choosing deceit as he gloats.

Destruction is of our own construct coveting our neighbors' wealth we fall prey to the raptor.

Soaring wings lifted by lusts of power, money burns with a hot fire we have elected our own captor

Worshiped, saluted, chosen by the majority self-imposed slavery for our own greed ever we seek.

Images of wealth for all, history repeated, Hitler reborn, Caligula enthroned anew death's reek.

Our abyss grows as we pour efforts into immoral endeavors pursuing the ease of debauchery.

We care for only ourselves who can get us there more quickly no debt too great for our voracity.

Enlightenment we claim as into the dark ages we plunge blindly delving into 2000 years past.

Concealed easily from those who choose not to see our 239th year may very well be our last.

Quickly seek our hearts' desires through perversions seductions we delve building decadence.

The lock to our prison freely clicked, chosen, embraced into lusts of spreading precedence.

Undone

We are undone by acts of attrition against those who hold the faith. We are undone by failure to give aid to those who suffer. We are undone by bearing false witness against the innocent. We are undone by worshipping the gods of greed. We are undone by fornicating with the harlots of malice. We are undone by coveting the spoils of our neighbor's endeavors. We are undone by the labors of fruitless striving for mounds of tarnished treasure. We are undone by the pursuits of the craven images of deceit. We are undone using the name of God for the cursing of our enemies. We are undone by the disobedience against the instruction of our parents. We are undone by the murder of hatred against those who oppose our will. We are undone by the theft of our children's inheritances. Our inequity is undone by the repentant opening the doors of faith. Our damnation is undone by grace through faith. Our blackened hearts are undone by the white washing of Jesus' blood. Our hate is undone by the pure love of forgiveness. Our guilt is undone by the acceptance of debts paid by riven body of our Redeemer.

Urgency

The walk of life's journey nears the end of the path and weary feet stumble at the brink of the abyss as the harps play a derelict litany. Directives disregarded chew up the pavement of smooth transitions with a flute's sharp cries. Into the silent nights strong hands muffle the ears of the unwilling against the warning bells' loud clanging chimes. The correction rod of discipline beat at the layered dust of the stubborn whose crusted rugs are the result of wayward dancing to the piper's seductions. The Judge tarries for a season's season stretching opportunity for repentances to those who listen to angel choruses. Written in words of instruction the assembling of obedience is a matter of perseverance against the tantalizing cabaret of burlesque. The teachings of the wise brush the coat tails of the preoccupied with the tapping of the drums of hope. The heralds of the ending of the age stand on the rivers of strife and proclaim the truth with the sounding of trumpets. The urgency of the final call peels out in R.S.V.P. laced announcements of the celebration of Love's triumphant orchestra of eternal life offers.

Useless Striving

Up at dawn the day to tread

Mind heavy weighed with thoughts of dread

All the chores from first to last

Reeling through mind with a fiery blast

Pulse in the head like a drummer's beat

Throbbing, throbbing from head to feet

One, two, three and four

Everywhere to look more and more

One brick at a time with a toss

Placed in a basket and promptly lost

Ever building with a feverish pace

A useless heap during the rat race

Hording temporary treasure untold

That which will tarnish, rot and mold

Step by without a glance

A child of God lost without a chance

Not even a kind word to share

Too busy with thoughts of work to care

Always striving, never achieving

Not enough sense to know the angels are grieving

When did I see you hungry and not feed you

The decades fly past, they are so few

When were you freezing and I gave you no coat

Lord, don't forsake me here in this brimstone moat.

Usurped

Pilfered quietly by the hands of deceit, an offer of awareness was made. Plucked by desire, the fruit of knowledge was consumed and life ceased. Pinched with the stones of guilt, eternity was terminated by jealousy. Embezzled by soft spoken words of the deceiver, faith fled screaming into the light. Purloined by fingers of delight, sin was clasped to the bosoms of the tempted and its cloying fragrance permeated the air. Filched from the purse of the righteous, sanctity was corrupted by the hands of the immoral. Pocketed by the greedy, abundance was diverted and the innocent were left to dearth. Taken without regard, the naïve were delivered into darkness. Lifted from the cradle of paradise, eyes were opened to the world of suffering. Robbed of fellowship, willful disobedience walked boldly into fig leaves and fell. Stolen by choice, the blameless became polluted and were purged. Raided by the unwitting, the pantry of life was emptied. Ransacked by the armies of odium, the city of peace was shattered. Ravaged by the lusts of the abhorrent, the virtuous opened the thighs of quilt and succumbed to evil desires. Wrecked by the derailment of the train of truth, lies proliferated chocking the vines of hope. Usurped from the hand of the Omniscient, knowledge became an unguided wrecking ball and destroyed the tower of love.

Veneer

A façade of piety veils the ravenous wolf's hungry eyed groping of innocence. A layer of cherry wood coats the scales of the serpent hiding the darkness from the light seekers. A pretense of virtue holds the hearts of the deceived in a grip of enthrallment. A show of prayers delights the prideful arms of pomp and circumstance. A guise of radiance shimmers over the black cloak of hate. A coating of makeup hides the sores of the unjust. A shroud of religion justifies the murderous intent of the corrupted. A pall of smoke conceals the consuming fires of the iniquitous' evil acts. A blanket of ash covers the rock piles of attrition. A mask of obedience disguises the deeds of the rebellious. A mantle of oak sits above the soot of waywardness. A sheet of ivory wraps the exploits of the foolish in layers of ignorance. The veneer must be shed down to the bones and blood of a contrite heart before the door of salvation is opened.

Vigil

Quietly awaiting in the last midnight hour, expectantly the dawning is searched. Breath held in anticipation of the arrival the wakeful kneel in hope. Hands quiver as wicks are trimmed in preparation. Feet fly under the unprepared who become stricken in oil-less flight. Hope grows with the lateness of the hour. The reluctant Judge tarries, the chosen numbers have not yet been filled. Eyes seek out each new sound; attentively ears strain to catch the footfalls. Fingers nervously cling to the light, hopeful of the return. Toes curl in expectation of the Faithfull's reward. Knees lock in solid resolve of those who look forward to the return of truth. Vigilant steps keep pace with truth and prevail. The watchful enter in while the inattentive fall away captured by lies. The celebration begins as the last stray is gathered. The seduced yammer for equality with those whose vigil withstood temptations. The meek are gathered under the wings of the Dove of Peace and prosper. The haughty forsake truth to pursue their hearts' desires. Love's patience has ended with the final count's tally. Judgment descends upon the multitudes of oblivious deniers and they are snared by their own refusals of the truth.

Vista

The burden of truth is easily born on shoulders which are carried by faith. The weight of hope is as light as a feather floating on the breezes of love. The yoke of contrition is freeing to those who snap it in place with their own hand. The trials of a hard life hone the blades of recognition of instruction from above. The Word of salvation is translated for the ears of the repentant. The songs of the cherubim are joyous music to the ears of the steadfast. The twinkle of light shines boldly on the paths of the grace acceptors. The chain of love links all the flock into the corral of heaven. The mountains of sorrow are easily flown over on the wings of forgiveness. The sunset of struggles dawns on the vista of reward. The panorama of paradise awaits those who hold firm until the end.

Where Have all the Joys Gone?

Our days are filled with untold joy.
Sunshine a warm wind blowing what mores need by a young boy.
Slingshot and summertime are full of promise never ending possibility.
Old stones groan speaking the ancient tunes of their probability.
The trees sway and murmur voices not quite as old as the stone's.
Roots curled digging to a depth then back out drying up like the bones.
Leaves from last fall lie under an overhang a great burial ground.
Hands burrow first into the dirt then a crevasse, a nook treasures to be found.
Acorns and hickory nuts scooped up to hoard, pockets to fill.
A boy's day a battle a war are the pleasure today they fit the bill.
Running climbing a tree to scale a daily plan has no value at all.
A pirate's ship or a castle gate no limit the old rock face and endless wall.
A woodland boy has no worry of injury, blood or even life lost.
The day's fun a boy trails and tracks to find at any cost.
The pursuit of untold joys was such a simple hunt.
Young boys knew the path to confront.
A tortoise, a bug, a frog on a vine are all worth many an hour of time.
A stick a rock and a length of twine a boy could rival anything in Mother Goose's Rhyme.
Life is a joy we need only remember how; go back to youth if we can only see
Move passed the days worries and get back to the simple things, be free.
The joys haven't gone they are here to take.
Choose life, be true, make haste before it is too late.
Where have all the joys gone, we have posed?
Nowhere, I say it is we who fled many doors we have closed.
Where has all the fun been spent?

In our youth we explain as in our day we grumble but don't repent.

Our untold joys await round every corner and unopened door.

We need only see, grasp, and take opportunity offered nothing more.

Whittled

Carved into the heartwood of hope, the repentant are fashioned into useful witnesses. Pared into the grains of faith, the stalwart are etched into figures of truth. Inscribed into the knots of love, the sinful are transformed into figures of purity. Cut into the limbs of intercession, the reprobate are pardoned into freedom. Shaped with the drawing knife of transformation the errant are converted into righteousness. Etched into the oak of life, the aberrant have been grafted into the tree of the forgiven. Notched into the block of discipleship, the chosen are tasked with witnessing. Trimmed into the vine of fruitfulness, the heirs sow seeds of the good news. Shaved into the likeness of purity, the transgressors postulate the robes of the children. Whittled with the tools of instruction, the humble learn to impart declarations of grace before the fortresses of ignorance.

Wood Ash and Lye Soap

The sun was always bright the air always warm the pot crouched over the embers of the fire.

Wood ash was gathered, sifted finer than the finest flour, renderings made ready on the pyre.

Granny's secret ingredients were laid by in a paper sack hidden from any prying eye.

First one then a tother added stirring, bubbling, and steaming like the filling of a fine lemon pie.

The smells grew wafting upward with the steam ever thickening at each stir.

Wood ash and sitch ingredients at hand anything and everything made to stand, its soap sir.

The traveling salesman stopped by old mule at the gate his nose twitched a hot meal to be ete.

He'd spied the big pot by the smokehouse steaming and thought a good meal he'd get.

Rose petals wood ash and Lilac his nose finally discerned as I answered him again soap.

His disappointment was grand frown complete muttered a word obscene and turned, the dope.

If he'd only stuck round a moment you see, granny never turned a hungry soul from the door.

Plenty he'd been given 'n even more hot coffee 'n a filled paper sack for his empty belly sore.

But alas he weren't patient saw no quick sale here a poor widow's hovel he assessed no more.

He mounted he's ole mule doft he's fancy hat eyed my bare feet 'n said leave here son yer poor.

I eyed him a doubt'n as the ole mule took him on granddad round'n the corner doc's bag in hand.

I took the ole grey mare as granddad stepped down who wuz that he asked eye roving the land.

Some quack salesmen I reply with a grin didn't like granny's soap I expect as I led away ole Beck.

Back to table the men began to pile in, food was hep'd high 'n overflowed waited my turn by heck.

Xenolith

A ruby among the brimstones shining brightly out of inky despair, the Xenolith of hope shines a light of guidance. A diamond isolated in the seam of coal of hate, the Xenolith of love binds the receptive. A gold nugget buried in the mountainous refuse of lewdness; the Xenolith of purity beckons the innocent. A sapphire flung into the quarry of inequity; the Xenolith of justice balances the scales for the forgiven. A pearl cast into the swine sty of the nefarious, the Xenolith of righteousness consumes the guilt of the grace seekers. A topaz trodden into the hard packed clay of the road to perdition, the Xenolith of warning utters dire words of an impending precipice to the abyss. A silver thread in the tapestry of the cast stones of condemnation, the Xenolith of forgiveness opens the eyes of the accusers. An emerald embedded in the quagmire of transgression; the Xenolith of obedience pardons the repentant. An amethyst bulldozed into the landfill of squandered opportunity; the Xenolith of resurrection gives new life to the faithful. An opal spiked into the cross of guilty pebbles, the Xenolith of paid debts removes the consequences of sin. A bloodstone fallen into the debris of Calvary; the Xenolith of intercession stands defending His sheep against the testimonies of the malicious prosecutor.

Xylem

My sap drips mingling with drops of blood from the hands of the Innocent. My heartwood beats in anguish to the injustice of a death undeserved. My leaves have fallen as the tears of the mourning are shed. My limbs quake in the tempest of shouts from the wicked. My bark is become stained with the crimson payment for the lost. My roots are set in the stones of the tomb readied gallows. My pith has been pierced by the spikes of hate. My foliage of life has been stripped by the hands of the ignorant. My branches have been dispersed offered unto the whole earth. My core has been riven by fiendish lusts of arrogant power-mongers. My veins have been stripped by the shards of lies flung in the words of hypocrisy. My xylem has been ruptured by those who fear Love.

Yearning

Thirst for truth has succumbed to the vortex of the drain of the deceived. Hunger for life has been devoured by the wolves of the ravenous hordes of acceptance. The ache for love has been massaged away by the fingers of the sexually immoral. The desire for hope has been sated by the pandering to debauched demands of purity. The yen for redemption has been nailed to the tree of fruitless indulgences. The longing for faith has been perverted into self-reliant fabrications of the damned. The zeal for righteousness has been redirected into acts of hate mongering murderers. The fervor to carry the gospel to the ignorant has been burned away by the Pharisees of greed. The enthusiasm for succor has been stabbed by the swords of pride. The passion for forgiveness has been skewered by the spikes of the offended. The eagerness for inclusion has been extended by the hands of the nefarious. The craving for Christ has been smothered by the masks of the addiction cartels. The yearning for God has been robbed from the ignorant by the lies of science. Sought we refuse to be found, courted we refuse to be wooed, offered grace we refuse to be redeemed, given death we refuse to accept life all in the name of a lie.

Yet

The guilty's trial is scheduled, yet their pardon they refuse. The indictment has been returned, yet the culpable ignore intercession. The accusations are verified by witnesses, yet the liable deny the truth of their guilt. The charges are innumerable, yet the blame is not accepted. The incriminations weigh heavy on the shoulders of the blameworthy, yet they point fingers at the innocent. The allegations are proved, yet the hypocrite declares his innocence. The offenses are without defense, yet the sinner rationalizes his actions. The crimes are horrific, yet the murderer declares they are justified. The transgressions are willful, yet the adulterer clings to his seductions. The indulgences were without ending, yet the greedy vow they have consumed only their fair share. The felonies are multiplied, yet the lawbreakers perjure their testimony. The sins are overwhelming, yet the unrepentant spit in the blood of Love.

Yoke

The yoke of love binds the necks of the oxen of submission into the reins of freedom. The yoke of fellowship binds the strength of the steadfast into the harness of the Purveyor of truth. The yoke of hope binds the weakness of faith into the gears of unchanging guidance. The yoke of forgiveness binds the sinful into the doubletree of pardon. The yoke of discipleship binds the witnesses of truth into the collar pad of the testimonies of the gospel. The yoke of morality binds the repentant into the belly straps of the righteous. The yoke of resurrection binds the door openers into the halter of the flock of the Redeemer. The yoke of arbitration binds the bridles of the guilty to the hands of the Arbitrator. The yoke of accepted sacrifice splices the debtors into the chain of the Debt payer. The yoke of eternity opens wide to accept the defendants holding tightly to the hands of their Liberator. The yoke of God must be lifted by the hands of willingness and clamped about their necks in obedience and humbleness.

Made in the USA
Columbia, SC
16 July 2024

994a3c2a-fa27-473c-97a6-d4d5c0a549deR01